The Hope That Kills Us

An Anthology of Scottish Football Fiction

The Hope That Kills Us

An Anthology of Scottish Football Fiction

Edited by **Adrian Searle**

Produced by **Freight**
With assistance from Arts & Business

for

FREIGHT

Published by Polygon
West Newington House
10 Newington Road
Edinburgh

ISBN 1 904598 00 5

First Published by Freight 2002
Published by Polygon 2003

A CIP catalogue record for this book is
available from The British Library

Typeset in Claremont
Printed by Creative Print & Design, Ebbw Vale, Wales

Contents

Preface

The Hope That Kills Us is the first ever anthology dedicated exclusively to Scottish football fiction. It was first published in hardback in December 2002 by Freight, the Glasgow based design consultancy, a self-commissioned project bringing together design, writing, football and photography.

Eight leading Scottish writers were commissioned to provide stories, either directly on indirectly, about our beautiful game. Some we knew well, others were introduced to us for the first time.

As part of the project, we wanted to give fans a voice and highlight previously unpublished Scottish writers. We visited writing groups in Easterhouse, HM Prison Glenochil, Perth and the Universities of Glasgow, Strathclyde and Edinburgh. From these workshops and through word of mouth we received around fifty submissions from all over the country, which together scrutinised Scottish football from an extraordinary number of angles. In the end, after a lengthy process and a great deal of deliberation, five additional short stories were selected for publication.

Arts & Business were key in encouraging Freight's support of new Scottish writing through the development of this book. Their financial assistance and advice proved invaluable.

We are delighted that Polygon agreed to further extend the life of *The Hope That Kills Us*. The publication of this paperback will highlight some of Scotland's best writers to a wider audience. In addition to the original thirteen authors included in the first edition, we've added two further stories. Brian Hennigan's satire, *The Tomintoul Deliverance*, was commissioned specifically for the new edition while *A Belfast Memory* by Bernard MacLaverty is the only story in the anthology to have been published elsewhere, previously appearing in *Celtic View* and *The Scotsman*. But we liked it so much we couldn't leave it out.

All photography included here is part of a much larger work by New York-based Scottish photographer, Paul Thorburn. Paul completed a major photo essay on Scottish football across five separate themes which was included in the first edition of *The Hope That Kills Us*. Further details can be obtained from www.freightdesign.co.uk.

Scottish football is the weirdest of organisms, simultaneously proving compelling and repulsive in equal measure. The range of participants, observers, experience and emotion is so broad that *The Hope That Kills Us* only begins to convey some kind of outline to its shape and texture. However, we hope that for those who share our mania, and for many that don't, this book proves to be as pleasurable, stimulating and ultimately satisfying as a steak pie from Ochilview on a freezing Saturday in January.

Adrian Searle
Director, Freight
October 2003

Foreword

"Anybody who says he disnae like football is a lyin' bastard".

These simple and imaginative words stalk many of the short stories in this collection. In fact, they are such a simple and eloquent summary of the Scottish experience, that it should be our national motto. Forget France's philosophical journey through egalite, liberte and fraternity or England's pompous land of hope and glory. There is nothing intrinsically wrong with aspiring to Himalayan values like freedom and glory – but they seem such a difficult mountain to climb and such evasive virtues to hold on to.

Personally I would prefer Scotland to identify a philosophy that we could universally achieve. Anybody who disnae like football is a lyin bastard – is a much more primal and honest thought. It is so much easier to live up to.

The words appear in Colin Clark's *The Last Man Left in Scotland,* the story of Pasty Hastie, a bullied schoolboy who plays the clarinet and doesn't like football. In the prophetic words of the author, is he "askin for trouble?" It is hardly surprising that trouble duly follows. Hastie ends up being jailed for five years for exposing himself, and inadvertently forces a bus to plough into a Nissan Micra in a horrendous local accident. The moral is simple – in Scotland it's simply safer to like football. Football's centrality to popular experience recurs like a leit-motif on virtually every page, especially those written by women. Denise Mina, Linda Cracknell and Laura Hird all contribute to the collection drawn to the subject of football because it is a route of entry to other creative and emotional challenges, they explore everything from bigotry to poverty, from anger to self-doubt and love – all the way back to loveless family life.

The theme that dominates even more than football is memory. The past, and particularly the lived and experiential past of modern Scotland, infects the stories like an old coat that can never be comfortably discarded. In Iain Maloney's *Football Scarves and Richard Kimble* it is back to childhood and a rights of passage that binds the old-firm and an American TV series, The Fugitive, together.

For the formidable Alan Spence it is a trip to Brazil to see Flamengo play Palmeiras in a deserted Maracana stadium. Somehow, even here at the ethereal home of football, the brilliant stench of Scotland cannot be fully evaporated.

Des Dillon provides a lovingly crafted life of the Heatherstone brothers, two Celtic fans who live together on a farm in Galloway, where every person is a contemplation, and where waiting is an art form.

There is something in the solitariness of Dillon's landscape that touches the same emotions as Paul Thorburn's still lives, a series of quiet and reflective photographs of goal-posts. These simple white rectangular shapes dominate the landscape throughout Scotland, in snow, in bleak grey nights, on housing schemes and on wasted rural land. It is remarkable how these photographs support the central thesis of this book – that Scotland cannot escape its self-consuming passion for football.

One of the most appealing things about micro-stories in the collection is that they can be like a poem or a favourite song – something you are happy to revisit time and time again. I found myself treating Jim Carruther's *The Cherrypicker* almost like a compact disc, pressing rewind and reading again. It is painfully short, the story of an unnamed narrator grieving the death of his grandfather.

He knows his grand-dad could play a bit and came from the old mining village of Glenbuck in Ayrshire. This famously was the home of the eloquent Glenbuck Cherrypickers, the team that Bill Shankly played for before his rise to managerial god at Liverpool. The name is such a poetic non-sequitar in an area gripped by an ugly poverty. But picking through his grand-father's life the narrator finds nothing to connect the old man to the Cherrypickers. There is no card from Liverpool, no requiem from old team-mates and the nagging doubt that maybe he made it all up. All that is left at the end is Glenbuck itself, now virtually extinct and invisible. If ever there was a short epithet to Scottish mining it is this fascinating story.

One of the dispiriting things about memory is its inexorable connection with the past – a past often best forgotten. Many of these stories describe a loss – the loss of community in central Scotland, the loss of childhood innocence, and the loss of a time when football was pure. At times this is a highly romanticised vision, a Scottish condition, that we seem incapable of overcoming.

But there is also a real sense that something deep has been forsaken, a time when Scotland was relevant and a time when pure football was played out on ashen pitches and dark streets. A time when balls could talk.

In that respect, this is a largely a class specific view of Scotland. It is working class. Of course, there are small detours to rural and small town Scotland, and through the brilliantly observed mind of Denise Mina we are taken on a tour of a nouveau riche gangster's house before the real violence begins. But the metaphors and the undercurrents of incoherent rage always return back to the Scotland of the central belt. Back to an era of failed and degraded industry. Back to basics.

If you live in Scotland and don't like football then there is every possibility you will not like this book. There is every possibility you are also a lying bastard. Lie to your friends, lie to your family but why lie to yourself? It is the hope that kills us.

If you are only visiting Scotland, and have stumbled on this book by chance, you may be surprised that a country can unite so many seemingly contradictory emotions around a game. Try not to interpret this in any rational way – that would be the wrong way of reading.

Think more of magical realism played out in replica shirts – when this football is described it is pure, it is magical and often it is exquisite. Balls swerve deceptively, keepers are chipped, and defences are split with hairline passes. This is the Scotland of the creative imagination – a small nation at its self-deluding best. Magic. But never far from a more painful social realism.

Or better still think of these stories as a journey through a rich, volatile and shifting language, words trying to grasp the enigmas of a nation. Andrew C Ferguson's *Nae Cunt Said Anyhin,* is, for example, an earthy story about a Fife footballer's rise and fall. It is witheringly accurate about the state of Scottish football. His central character, a self-destructive genius who can make love to leather, eventually gets a game for Scotland. Once this meant something but for the writer's generation – the Scottish team is "so shite even he can't make a difference". Scotland, as the phrase would have it, couldn't score on the Loveboat.

Alan Bisset, offers us a more poetic vision of the game and its grip on the Scottish psyche – for him, it's "the whole world crammed intae a wee box that wis a summer's day." Anyone who doesn't want to peek into that worldly box cannot like football.

Lying bastard.

Stuart Cosgrove
is the presenter of BBC's Scotland Off the Ball

The Thing About Brazil

Alan Spence

legs frozen
pink and stinging,
his studs
catching on the
hard-frozen grass

Flying down to Rio. He looked out the window – there should be a line of tap dancers high stepping it along the wing. But no. Just the dark, and the wing bucking and wobbling that way he always found unsettling, the light flashing trippy patterns on the vapour clouds rushing past.

He pulled down the buff plastic blind. Nothing to see. And nothing on the screen, except the endlessly updated statistics. Distance to destination. Time at destination. Altitude. Outside temperature. Impossible not to watch it, desperately willing the time to pass.

Way down among Brazilians, coffee beans grow by the millions. Altitude 30,000 feet. Outside temperature, minus 30 degrees. A bit tricky for the wing-dancing. His feet were twitchy, agitated. He needed to re-hydrate. A politician's daughter was accused of drinking water. This would be him for the whole time he was here, the place defined by a back catalogue of movies and old songs. Desafinado. Slightly out of tune, right enough.

He rubbed his face, the skin dried out, roughness of stubble, eyes tired and gritty. Breathed the stale air. Looked up at the screen again and the stats had been replaced by the map showing where they were. The tiny wee plane had moved a millimetre since the last time it appeared. And he was suddenly overwhelmed by a sense of scale, felt how huge this country actually was. Scotland would fit into that couple of inches along the coast. The vastness numbed him, a taste like iron in his mouth.

Waking in the middle of the night, no idea who he was, or where. Not home, the window was on the wrong side. And he was too hot. He threw off the covers, got his feet out and onto the floor, stood up, unsteady. The dark shapes resolved into the contours of the room. He found the switch on the bedside lamp, clicked it on. Remembered. The usual characterless hotel space, blandly impersonal. Could be anywhere, except for the pictures on the wall, samba dancers, the statue of Christ the Redeemer overlooking the city, arms outstretched.

He crossed to the window, pulled open the curtains. Pressed up close and shielded his eyes to squint out. Fifteen floors down he could just make out a curve of beach, the sea crashing in almost soundless, shut off by the double-glazing. Further round the great sweep of the shore and the lights of other hotels. That would be Ipanema, and beyond, the Copacabana.

Stepping back he saw himself reflected, the room behind him a capsule in space. Felt the emptiness again, closed the curtains, caught for a moment their faint fusty smell.

At first light he went down to the beach, breathed deep. The wash of the waves felt healing, brought ease. He walked along just above the tide lapping in, his sandalled feet sinking at every step. Even this early the sand was warm. He stopped at a small stream, followed it back up with his eyes. It flowed down from the hill that towered behind the hotel. The hillside was sheer, at some points almost a cliff face, and all the way up were houses and shacks, huddled, ramshackle, clinging on. These were the *favelas* he'd read about, clusters of hovels with no street names or numbers. The stream was probably pure sewage. He turned and headed back to the hotel.

Breakfast was lavish. He loaded his plate with fresh fruit – pineapple, mango, papaya – and was looking for a place to sit when the young Englishman caught his eye.

'Morning.'

He'd come off the same flight, checked in at the same time, was here for a conference.

'Hi,' he said, nodding.

'Steve,' said the Englishman.

'Andrew.'

They found a table by the window, waited a moment while the waiter cleared it.

Steve had stacked his plate with a fry-up, bacon and sausage, fried egg.

'Full English!' he said.

'I'll get some eggs after this,' said Andrew. 'Do me fine.'

'You sleep all right?'

'Not bad. Woke a bit early.'

'The way the jetlag works,' said Steve, dipping sausage into his egg yolk. 'You'll be knackered this afternoon.' He shoved the food in his mouth, swilled it down with tea. 'Your room on this side?'

'Yeah. Great view.'

'Safer too.'

'How come?'

'I've heard the folks who live on the hill take the occasional potshot at the windows.'

'Jesus!'

'Can't be too careful.'

'Same old story. These folk have nothing. Zero. Nada. As far as they're concerned we've got the lot.'

'Sounds like you should be talking to this conference!'

'Thanks but no thanks. What's it about?'

'Globalisation, in its many guises. My session's on ethical banking.'

'Nice work!'

'Politically it's important to be holding it here.'

'I'm sure.'

Steve squinted at him, weighing him up. 'What line of work you in yourself?'

'Academia. I teach literature.'

'Nice work!'

'Sometimes!'

'So what brings you here?'

'Oh, just getting away. Taking a sabbatical. I needed a break.'

'From what?'

'Long story.'

'Fine.' Steve left a pause, poured himself more tea. 'Why Brazil?'

He laughed. 'Blame Pele! Or Garrincha!'

'Football! I should have known!'

'How?'

'You're Scottish!'

'Fair cop. But you know how something gets hold of you. I've always fancied coming here.'

'Good call. With the pollution and the drug gangs and the AIDS and the muggings and the random shootings.' He laughed again. 'Don't look so serious! It's a great place! Just have to keep your wits about you, that's all.'

He had to get to a bank, change some money, so he took a taxi down to Leblon. He still felt out of sync, disembodied, saw everything sharp and clear but with a kind of detachment. He sat for an hour at a pavement cafe, people-watching over two cups of dark bitter coffee that kick-started his nervous system, sent him out grinning into the street. They got an awful lot of coffee in Brazil.

When he got back to the hotel, he saw Steve again, in the lobby.

'Not conferencing?'

'Doesn't start till tomorrow, thank God. But listen, there's a big game at the Maracana tonight. Flamengo and Palmeiras, some cup tie. This guy at the desk can get tickets.'

'How much?'

'Works out about twenty quid a head. Includes a bus there and back.'

'Jesus, that's not bad.'

'That's what I thought. Are you in?'

'Absolutely. Yes. Aye.'

His guidebook had advice on going to the game.

Buy a ticket in advance for the *arquibandadas,* the seated terraces.

Do not stray into the *geral* or standing area.

Do not carry valuables or wear a watch.

Do not be tempted to buy a club shirt.

'Fuckin hell,' said Steve. 'Sounds worse than Millwall!'

Andrew flipped through the book, read something that made him laugh out loud.

Steve looked up. 'What?'

'Says in here there's a convent on the outskirts of town has a statue to somebody called Wild Jock of Skelater!'

'Ancestor of yours?'

'Scottish soldier of fortune, fought for the Portuguese in the Napoleonic Wars.'

'Bloody Scots got everywhere.'

'The original Tartan Army! Can just see him, a cross between Braveheart and the janny in The Simpsons!'

He read on. 'Thing is, if I've got this right, when he died they carried on paying a salary to his statue. The money went to the convent.'

'You couldn't make that up.'

'Magic realism!'

'Is that what it is?'

The bus picked them up outside the hotel, an hour before kick-off. They paid the driver, sat at the front.

Here we go.

'Like being a kid!' he said, exhilarated. 'Supporters bus to away games.'

'Jeez!' said Steve. 'You were seriously into this shit!'

'And you weren't?'

'Followed Man U from a distance. But supporters buses? Away games? That's way too real!'

Waiting for his father outside the pub in Scotland Street, across the road from Howdens. Sometimes the old man would come straight off an overtime shift on the Saturday morning, go straight in to the pub and drink till it was time to leave for the game. Andrew waited for ever outside on the pavement till the bus pulled up and the men came spilling out of the bar, reeking of beer and smoke. The warm fug engulfed him as his father ruffled his hair, swung a joke punch at him, bobbing and weaving.

'Awright wee man?'

'Fine, Da.'

And so he was, as he thud thud thudded his feet on the floor of the bus, sang *Follow Follow* and *No Surrender* all the way to Kilmarnock, or Motherwell, or Airdrie. Everywhere, anywhere. Surrender or you'll die. Was that really what they sang? The People.

The bus stopped at four or five other hotels along the Copacabana, picked up more passengers, all middle aged, European, male. Beerbellies bulged under replica strips, Bayern Munich, AC Milan. The bus filled with Eurobabble as they swung away from the waterfront, on through an area that was more industrial, shabby factories and warehouses. They stopped in a back-up of traffic outside one old building, derelict and run-down. But work was going on inside, and through sparks and flashing arc lights a huge carnival head grinned out, a cartoon bear. Along one wall was a line of graffiti, a dollar sign morphing into a swastika.

The stadium, seen close up, was a great grey mass of ageing concrete. It smelled damp. Inside, on the concourse, a couple of young boys were set up at a table, selling replica strips. Flamengo colours, red and black, the classic Brazil jersey, yellow with the green trim, the away strip in royal blue.

'Remember what your guidebook said.' Steve wagged a finger at him. 'Thou shalt not buy a club shirt.'

'National colours should be safe enough.'

'Unless you run into some mental Argentinian.'

'And if my arithmetic's right, these are about a fiver each. Buy them in town and they're forty quid.'

'Yeah,' said Steve, 'for the genuine article.' He sifted the material. 'These are cheap nylon rip-offs.'

'They're a fiver!'

He bought one of each, one yellow, one blue, both with the number 9 and RONALDO on the back.

'You're just a big kid!' said Steve.

Andrew peeled off his t-shirt, stuffed it in the plastic bag with the blue jersey, pulled on the yellow one over his head.

'Yes!'

He ran up the steps to the terracing.

Always that moment of exhilaration, coming up the steps at Ibrox, the sudden vibrant intensity of the bright green grass, the vividness of the jerseys against it, the deep blue, the yellow and red, the claret and amber. Always the same smells in the open air, cigarettes and brylcreem, beer and sweat and carbolic soap. Always the same songs on the tannoy, *Song of the Clyde*, *Let The Great Big World Keep Turning*. These days the smells were Givenchy and Calvin Klein, and the p.a. played Tina Turner as the teams ran out. Simply the Best.

But the crowd still added their own coda. Tina belted out, *I see the star of every night and day*. And the crowd roared back, *Fuck the Pope and the IRA*.

The Maracana looked almost empty, nobody at all in the upper tiers, huge gaps down below.

'I thought it would be packed,' he said, a bit disappointed.

'Well, it holds two hundred thousand,' said Steve. 'So even quarter full would be a fair crowd.'

He shrugged. 'Guess so.'

They found their seats, shoved their way along the row. The teams were already out, Flamengo in their red and black, Palmeiras all in green.

Andrew joined in the roar as they kicked off. He megaphoned his hands. 'Flamengo!'

'Taking sides already?' said Steve.

'They are the home team. Might be politic! And you've got to support somebody!'

'Why?'

'Come on! It's no fun if you don't care!'

'I don't see that it matters.'

'Might as well play that Zen football I read about. No goals. I mean, what's the point? It's perverted!'

Palmeiras were on the attack, down the near side, the right wing. A flick inside, the midfielder running onto it, a quick shimmy, double shuffle past two defenders, a languid cross to the edge of the box, big striker nodding it down, a lunged clearance breaking to the same midfielder who curled it, looping and dipping into the far corner of the net.

There was a deep muffled wounded noise from around the ground, a burst of localised cheering from behind the goal.

'Jesus Christ!' said Andrew. 'What a shot!'

'I thought you were supporting the locals?' said Steve.

'Doesn't mean I can't appreciate a thing of beauty.'

The scorer ran towards the corner flag, did a handstand and sprung right over onto his feet again in sheer acrobatic exuberance.

'Asprilla used to do that when he played for Newcastle,' said Andrew.

An old guy in front of them turned round, said, '*Sim*, Asprilla.'

'You mean that's him? Faustino Asprilla?'

The old guy nodded. *'Sim.'*

'Bloody hell!' He punched Steve on the arm. 'Isn't that amazing?'

There was a rumble of noise from behind the goal, drums beating out samba rhythm, a couple of hundred supporters in green being marshalled onto the terraces by police. Then there was a surge from further over, a section of the Flamengo crowd rushing at the invaders, hurling themselves against the fence that separated them.

Andrew looked across, quizzical, at their bus driver, sitting at the end of the row.

The man shrugged. 'Is the Palmeiras supporters. I think maybe their buses came late from Sao Paolo. And you know, the Cariocas and the Paolistas are not the best of friends.'

'Right.'

The game flowed on.

By halftime it was 2–2 and they were up out of their seats, standing with a few others at a rail along the front of the terrace.

'More like the thing,' he said. 'They should still have standing areas back home.'

Below them was a sheer drop into a channel that ran round the whole ground, like a moat that had been drained. On the other side of it were the open terracings, the *geral,* the main mass of supporters packed in. The energy level down there was altogether different, anarchic and wild. The samba beat pulsed, and the crowd moved to it, danced and chanted and jabbed their fists in the air. A group of young boys turned and yelled up at them, laughed. Andrew waved back, called out 'Flamengo!' and they laughed even more.

The whole of the second half, they shouted and gestured up at them. At first it seemed good-natured, inclusive. But as the game went on it became more aggressive, mocking. Towards the end, something white was thrown in their direction, flashed past, hit the steps just behind them. They looked round, saw a dead chicken, splattered on the concrete.

'Something to do with Macumba,' said Steve. 'Voodoo. Bad magic.'

'Jesus!'

Into the last five minutes, the score was 3–3 and Flamengo had a corner. Their lumbering striker timed his jump, got a touch and nodded it over the line.

'Yes!'

Andrew roared, thumped Steve on the back. The crowd down below went manic, pogoed up and down. A few of them yelled up again, gave them the finger. One shoved his hand down the front of his trackpants, mimed groping himself, thrusting his hips at them, his tongue hanging out.

'Don't fancy yours much!' said Steve.

Back on the bus, two of the Germans had taken the front seats, stared grimly straight ahead.

'Talk about racial stereotypes!' said Andrew.

They pulled out into slow traffic, easing along through the crowds on foot swarming away from the ground. He momentarily caught the eye of a young girl wearing a yellow jersey like his own. He pointed to the badge over his heart. CBF. She laughed and blew him a kiss. And at the same moment there was a crash from the other side of the bus, and a rock smashed through the window, showering the Germans with shattered glass.

'Fuckin hell!' said Steve as the driver jammed on the brakes. It was unreal, dreamlike, the crowds surging and dancing past, upbeat, the barrage of noise from traffic backed up behind them. The driver made sure the Germans weren't badly hurt, just a few cuts to their arms, thrown up in reflex to protect themselves. They didn't want to go to hospital, just to get back to their hotel as quickly as possible. A motorcycle cop pulled over and took some details. But nobody had seen who did it, just the rock hitting the glass, the window imploding in smithereens. The cop put away his notebook, revved up his bike and led them out onto the highway.

Back at the hotel, they sat drinking in the bar.

'You know,' said Steve, 'that could have been us, sat in that front seat.'

Andrew raised his glass. 'Deutschland uber alles!'

Steve laughed. 'Couldn't have happened to a nicer couple of blokes!'

'Achtung, baby!'

'What a night, eh? Welcome to Rio!'

'Some game, though!' said Andrew. 'I mean, the level of skill was just phenomenal.'

'The business.'

'That's the thing about Brazil. They took it to another level. *Jogo bonito.* The beautiful game. That's why we love them in Scotland. We still value that...*quality*.'

Steve spluttered. 'In your dreams!'

'Well, that's still something. We can still aspire.'

'Sad!'

'We've had guys that could play at that level. Jim Baxter. Denis Law. Kenny Dalglish.'

'To name but three! In what? Thirty years?'

'Okay, Brazil are in a different league. But we've had our moments against them.'

Billy Bremner failing to connect from six inches out. David Narey's toe-poke provoking four goals in retribution for daring to score first. John Collins' cheeky penalty before Rivaldo took them apart.

'Get real!' said Steve.

'Ach! Why would I want to do that?'

'We taught these people all they know,' said Steve. 'You know that curved free kick, *supposedly* a Brazilian speciality? Well Pele called that kick an *English*. So there!'

'Full English! Ach, you're making that up!'

'I am not!'

'Listen, it's your round!' He checked his watch. 'I should phone home, talk to my son.'

'You've got a son?' said Steve. 'Cool!'

'Ach, it's not exactly a Nick Hornby scenario. I mean, he doesn't even like football!'

'How old is he?' said Steve.

'Sixteen. His mother and I aren't together anymore.'

'Tough.'

'Hey, stuff happens. She's with another guy.'

'Can't be easy.'

'No.'

'Is that what you were getting away from?'

'Maybe. Also my old man died a month ago.'

'Sorry.'

'He was old. It was time.'

'But still.'

'Yeah. Still.'

'Listen,' said Steve. 'If you're phoning, use this.' He handed him a card with two numbers on it. 'Call the first number, and when they ask for your code, key in the second. It connects you for the cost of a local call. I spoke to my girlfriend this morning, and it only cost a quid for half an hour.'

'Are you sure?'

'Perks of the job.'

'Cheers.'

He got through first time. Jake the new guy answered, and put him on to Ann, who asked if he was drunk and said Jamie was watching TV.

'For God's sake,' he said. 'I'm phoning from Brazil!'

'I'll see if he wants to talk to you.' She clacked the receiver down on the tabletop. He could hear their voices through the crackle and hiss on the line and, as backdrop, the TV not turned down. When Jamie came to the phone there was annoyance in his voice, a strained patience.

'Hi, Dad.'

'Hi Jamie! You all right?'

'Fine. It's just, this is bad timing. Buffy's kicking the shit out a nest of vampires.'

'I was at the Maracana tonight.'

'Didn't know you were into clubbing!'

'You winding me up?'

The boy let out a distracted Oh!

'You all right?'

'Yeah. She just did a spectacular backflip and took out two demons.'

'Somebody smashed the window of our bus and the supporters throw dead chickens it's something to do with voodoo and right behind our hotel is the biggest slum in Rio and it's like a complete no go area.'

'So don't go there, dad. *Duh!*'

'Right.'

'Take it easy.'

'Yeah. You too.'

A click then the buzz of the dialing tone. Don't go there. Right.

Steve asked if he'd got through.

'The wee bastard was watching Buffy. Didn't want to know.'

'Hard to compete,' said Steve.

He was suddenly tired beyond belief.

'Need some kip myself,' said Steve. 'Conference starts tomorrow.'

'Got to sort out the world.'

'Big time!'

'Cancel the Debt. Would do for starters.'

'Unfortunately it's not as simple as that.'

'Nothing ever is.' He finished his drink, looked round. 'Ach!'

He slept late, woke groggy, the jetlag finally kicking in. He'd just be over it and it would be time to go home, back to what passed for reality. He took it easy, lazed the day away by the hotel pool, dozing in the heat, letting the prattle and chatter wash over him, hearing behind it the shoosh of the ocean. In the late afternoon he swam in the pool, a few short lengths. Revived, he decided to head out, catch the last of the day.

He put on the other jersey he'd bought at the game, the away strip, royal blue. Pulled on a pair of baggy beach shorts, his old adidas trainers. Checked himself in the mirror. The Men's Health magazine he'd bought to read on the plane was full of articles like Bust That Gut! Totally Ripped Abs. He lifted the jersey, slapped the flab. A walk along the beach would be a good start, down to the main drag and along to Copacabana.

The full strip his father had bought him that Christmas, folded in its own box, the white shorts, red and black socks, the blue blue jersey, shortsleeved, in softest cotton with the white v-neck. He'd worn it on Christmas morning, pulled on old clothes over it and headed out to the park with a couple of his pals, the heavy leather ball under his arm, his boots slung round his neck by the tied-together laces. It didn't matter how cold it was, he had to wear the strip. Pulled off the old jeans, the woolly jumper, put on the boots and ran about daft for an hour in clouds of his own breath, playing three-and-in, arms and legs frozen pink and stinging, his studs catching on the hard-frozen grass.

Every few yards along the way he passed a football game, or impossibly beautiful people playing frisbee or beach volleyball. He had never seen so many perfect bodies in his life. Tall and tanned and young and lovely. Ipanema. This was him, in Brazil. For real. What was he doing here? The late afternoon sun shimmered on the sea.

He prised off his trainers, walked barefoot on the warm sand.

Further along, the ball bounced over to him from a bunch of kids playing, no more than 10 or 11 years old, one or two adults in amongst them. He caught the ball on his right instep, brought it down, then flicked it up and volleyed it with his left. You never forget.

His father coaching him, teaching him how to kick with his left foot as well as his right. Wear a proper boot on the left, the weaker one. On the right wear an old beat-up sandshoe, the toes kicked out of it, so no temptation to use it on the hard heavy ball. Use the left to slam shot after shot against a wall, trap the rebound, hit it again, again, again.

One of the kids laughed, shouted 'Ronaldo!'

He gave a self-conscious shrug, waved back. One of the adults called out to him. 'You want to play? We have one man too less.'

'Sure,' he said. 'Yes! Why not?'

The last time he'd seen his father alive, a few weeks ago in the hospital, the old man shrunk in on himself, mind gone, barely able to recognise him at all. The young nurse had propped him up in bed, coaxed and cajoled a response out of him.

Hey Davie. Up Celtic!

Aye. Right up them!

As he was leaving, he turned in the doorway, said Cheerio, Da.

And the old man chanted it. *Cheerio! Cheerio! Cheerio!*

The way they do on the terracing when a man's sent off. Red card. Early bath.

The same tune as *Here we go!*

Here we go. Cheerio. All there was.

The kids were too good, too fast and skilled, too used to playing on the sand, adept at chesting it or keeping it in the air or taking it on the volley. And they didn't deign to go for the easy shot, the blootered clearance, the punt upfield. They stroked their passes, weighted to perfection. They feinted and dribbled, made space. And when they scored it was with a deft flick, a tap-in, a neat back-heel. They played with flair. *Jogo bonito.*

He stood with his hands on his knees, catching his breath, straightened up and looked about him, took it all in.

And all the world is football-shaped. It's just for me to kick in space.

Who sang that, way back?

He remembered. XTC!

And I've got one two three four five senses working overtime.

And what did XTC mean? And what ever became of them?

Cheerio. Cheerio. Cheerio.

His back was to the goal, the ball dropping towards him. And suddenly everything slowed down, was momentarily in slomo. He took his time. All the time in the world. The geometry of it was clear to him as he launched himself backwards, did a scissor-kick in mid-air and connected with the ball, sent it flashing over his head, his arms out to cushion the fall as he thudded down on the sand. And he laughed as he lay there, knew without looking it had beaten the keeper. And a little cheer went up from some of the kids.

'Bicicleta!'

'Pele!'

He picked himself up and wheeled, arms spread, taking the acclaim, the roar of the waves, and looking up saw the biggest fullest reddest moon he'd ever seen, rising in the still-blue sky, a ball of light hanging in space, and he jumped up and headed it, turned and punched the air.

'Yes!'

A Belfast Memory

Bernard MacLaverty

To Mr Tully here.
God guide your
golden boots.

Our two rented houses faced each other across the street – my father's at 73 and Aunt Cissy's at 54. There was another uncle, Father Barney, who used to call round most Sundays to Cissy's. In the evening they all played poker and Father Barney would drink whisky and do mock shouting and clowning. The others would roll their eyes. If the children were good and provided Father Barney wasn't 'beyond the beyonds' they were allowed to watch. My father always left early saying he had his work to go to in the morning. My mother said he just couldn't stand Uncle Barney any longer.

I knew my father's work had something to do with drawing and lettering. I'd found things in cupboards – small blocks of wood topped with grey zinc metal. If there was lettering on this metal it was always backwards, unable to be read. In cupboards there were pages of pink paper, thick as slices of bread, with lettering pressed into them and bulldog clips full of his newspaper adverts. At the moment he was illustrating a Bible for Schools. He'd shown me a drawing for the Cure at Capharnum and, as an exercise, made me read aloud the caption.

'They could not get in because the house was crowded out, even to the door. So they took the stretcher onto the roof, opened the tiles, and let the sick man down .'

I was about eight or nine at the time. It was dead easy.

It was a Sunday and felt like a Sunday. Family Favourites was on the wireless. My father sat beneath the window for the best light.

'What you doing ?'

He held up the drawing.

'Abraham and his son, Isaac,' he said. A man with a white beard beside a boy carrying a tied-up bundle of sticks. 'Where is the victim for the sacrifice? That's what the boy is saying.' My father put on a scary, deep voice and said, 'Little does he know...' He drew quietly for a while. The pen scratched against the paper and chinked in the ink bottle. He had a pad on the table and sometimes he made scratches on it. 'Just to get the nib going.' Sometimes the pen took up too much ink and he shook it a little. 'You're no good if you can't make something out of a blot.'

The hall door opened and footsteps came in off the street. My father stopped and looked up. It was my cousin, Brendan, who was a year and two months older than me. He was a good footballer.

' It's yourself, Brendy.'

Brendan stopped in the middle of the floor and said,

'Charlie Tully's in our house having a cup of tea.'

'Go on. Are you kidding?'

'No.'

My father gave a low whistle.

'This we will have to see.' He wiped his pen on a rag, then rinsed it in a jam jar of water. He blew on his drawing then folded the protective tissue over it.

'Come on.' All three of us went across the road. The only car parked on the street belonged to Father Barney.

'Did Barney bring him?' Brendan nodded.

'And Terry Lennon.'

Terry Lennon was a blind church organist. He had a great Lambeg drum of a belly with a waistcoat stretched tight over it. He would sit in the armchair by the fire smoking constantly, never taking the cigarette from between his lips. A lot of the time he stared up at the ceiling – his eyelids didn't quite shut and some of the white of his eye showed. Now and again he would run his fingers down the cigarette to dislodge the ash onto his waistcoat. Aunt Cissy called him Terry Lennon, the human ash-tray.

When we went in Terry Lennon was in his usual chair. Father Barney stood in front of the fire with his hands behind him. On the sofa was a man, still wearing his raincoat, drinking tea. His hair was parted in the middle. He was introduced to my father as Charlie Tully.

'You're welcome,' said my father. 'Is that sister of mine looking after you?'

Charlie Tully nodded.

'The best gingerbread in the northern hemisphere,' said Father Barney. 'That's what lured him here.'

'Where's the old man?' said my father.

'The last I saw of him was heading up to the lavatory with the Independent.'

'He'll be there for a week.' My father turned to the man in the pale raincoat.

'I bet he was delighted to see you Mr Tully – he's a bit of a fan.'

'Oh he was – he was.'

'So – how do you like Scotland?'

'It's a grand place.'

'Will Mr Tully have a cigarette?' Terry Lennon reached out in the general direction of the voice with his packet of Gallagher's Greens.

'Naw, he only smokes Gallagher's Blues,' said Aunt Cissy and everybody laughed.

'If you'll forgive me saying so Mr Tully,' said Terry Lennon, 'the football is not an interest of mine. You understand?'

'I do. You were making some sound with that organ this morning.'

'Loud ones are great.' Terry Lennon laughed. 'Or Bach. Bach is great for emptying the place for the next mass. The philistines flee.'

There was a ring at the door and Brendan went to answer it. When he came back he said it was Hugo looking for a drink of water.

'And run the tap for a while,' said Aunt Cissy laughing. 'Bring him in.'

'The more the merrier' said my father.

'Wait till you hear this, Mister Tully. Our Hugo.' Brendan went into the kitchen and ran the tap very fast into the sink. He carried a full cup into the room and called Hugo from the door. Hugo edged into the room and accepted the cup. There was silence and everybody watched him drink. Hugo was a serious young man who was trying to grow a beard.

Father Barney joined his hands behind his back and rose on his toes. He said,

'So you like to run the tap for a while?'

'Yes, Father.'

'And why's that?'

'The pipes here are lead. And lead is poison. Not good for the brain.'

'The Romans used a lot of lead piping,' said Father Barney, winking at Charlie. 'Smart boys, the Romans. They didn't do too badly.'

'No – you're right, Father. But maybe it's what destroyed their Empire,' said Hugo. 'Being reared to drink poison helps no one.'

Father Barney sucked in his cheeks and rolled his eyes.

'I need a whiskey after that slap down.' Aunt Cissy moved to the sideboard where the bottle was kept. 'Cissy fill her up with water, lead or no lead. Will anybody join me? What – no takers, at all?' He held up his glass. 'To Mister Tully here. God guide your golden boots.' Granda came downstairs and had to push the door open against the people inside.

'What am I missing?' he said.

'A drink,' said Father Barney. Granda looked around in mock amazement.

'He's getting no drink at this time of the day,' said Aunt Cissy. Granda was still wearing his dark Sunday suit and the waistcoat with his watch-chain looped across it. On his way to mass he wore a black bowler hat.

'It's getting a bit crowded in here,' Granda said, looking around the room. 'Reminds me of the day McCormack sang in our house in Antrim. There was that many in the room we had to open the windows so's the neighbours outside could hear him.'

'Count John McCormack?' said Charlie Tully.

'The very one.'

'How did the maestro end up in your house? '

'Oh, he was with Terry there, some organ recital.'

'And what did he sing?'

'Everything. Everything but the kitchen sink. Down by the Sally Gardens, I hear you calling me.'

'It was some show,' said Terry Lennon, putting his head back as if listening to it again.

'Would you credit that?' said Charlie. 'I met a man who knows Count John McCormack.'

There was a strange two note cry from the hallway, 'Yoo-hoo.'

'Corinna,' said Cissy and pulled a face. The door was pushed open and Corinna and her sister, Dinky, stood there.

'Full house the day,' said Corinna. She eased herself into the room.

Dinky remained just outside.

'The house is crowded out, even to the door,' said my father.

'Is there any chance of borrowing an egg, Cissy. I'd started the baking before I checked.' Cissy went into the kitchen and came back with an egg which she handed to Corinna.

'Thanks a million. You're too good.' Corinna stood with the egg between her finger and thumb. 'What's the occasion?' She vaguely indicated the full room.

'Charlie Tully,' said Cissy. 'This is Corinna Coyle. And her sister Dinky.' Cissy pointed over heads in the direction of the front hall. Dinky went up on her toes and smiled.

'A good looking man,' said Corinna.

'Worth eight thousand pounds in transfer fees,' said Father Barney.

'He's above rubies, Cissy. Above rubies.' And away she went with her egg and her sister.

'So,' said Granda, 'will we ever see Charlie Tully playing again on this side of the water?'

'Maybe.'

'Internationals,' said Hugo.

'But it's not the same thing,' said Granda, 'as watching a man playing week in, week out. That's the way you get the whole story.'

'There's talk of a charity game with the Belfast boys later in the year,' said Charlie.

'Belfast Celtic and Glasgow Celtic?' Granda was now leaning forward with his elbows on the table. 'There wouldn't be a foul from start to finish.'

'Where'd be the fun in that?' said Father Barney. 'Cissy, I'll have another one of those.' Cissy went to the sideboard and refilled the glass.

'Remember you've a car to drive.' Barney ignored her and pointed at my father,

'Johnny there would design you a program for that game. For nothing. He's a good artist.'

'Like yourself Charlie,' said Granda.

'Is that the kinda thing you do?' Charlie said.

'Yeah sure,' said my father. Barney started mock shouting as if he was selling programs outside the ground. Some of his whiskey slopped over the rim of the glass as he waved his arms. My father smiled.

'Have you been somewhere – before here ?'

'On a Sunday morning ?'

Barney looked over to Charlie Tully, 'Johnny does work for every charity in the town. The YP Pools, the St Vincent de Paul, the parish, even the bloody bishop – no friend of mine – as you well know – his bloody nibs. Your Grace.' He gave a little mock inclination of the head. Cissy ordered Brendan out of his chair and told Barney to sit and not be letting the side down.

'So Charlie,' said Granda, 'the truth from the insider – is there no chance of Belfast Celtic starting up again?'

'Not that I know of.'

'We gave in far too easily. In my day when somebody gave you a hiding, you fought back.'

'Aye, it's all up when your own side makes you the scape-goat,' said Aunty Cissy.

'I mean to say,' Granda's voice went up in pitch. 'What were they thinking of ?'

'The game of shame.'

'A crowd of bigots.'

'They came streaming onto that pitch like... like... bloody Indians.'

'Indians are good people,' said Hugo.

'...and they kicked poor Jimmy Jones half to death. Fractured his leg in five places. And him one of their own. It ended his career.'

'Take it easy, Da,' said Father Barney and slapped the arm of his chair.

'You were at the game?' said Charlie Tully.

'Aye and every other one they've ever played,' said Granda. ' I don't know what to do with myself on a Saturday afternoon now. I sometimes slip up to Cliftonville's ground but it's not the same thing. Solitude. It's well named.' Granda was shaking his head from side to side. 'I just do not understand it. What other bunch of people would do it? The board of directors,' he spat the words out. 'The team gets chased off the pitch, its players get kicked half to death and what do they do? Okay, we're going to close down the club. That'll teach you. In the name of Jesus...' Granda stopped talking because he was going to cry. He looked hard at the top of the window and he kept swallowing. Again and again. Nobody else said anything. 'Why should we be the ones sacrificed ? Is there no one on our side who has any guts at all?'

'Take it easy,' said my father. 'They have the sectarian poison in them.' He reached out and put his hand on Granda's shoulder. Shook him a little. Granda recovered himself a bit and said,

'It would put you in mind of the man who got a return ticket for the bus – then he had a row with the conductor – so, to get his own back, he walked home. That'll teach them.'

There were smiles at that. The room became silent.

'It was a great side,' said Charlie Tully at last. 'Kevin McAlinden, Johnny Campbell, Paddy Bonnar...'

'Aye.'

'And what a keeper Hugh Kelly was.'

'Aye and Bud Ahern...'

'Billy McMillan and Robin Lawlor.'

'Of course.'

'Jimmy Jones and Eddie McMorran and who else?'

'You've left out John Denver.'

'And the captain, Jackie Vernon.'

'And yourself, Charlie,' said Granda. 'Let's not forget yourself, maestro.'

Sometime later that year – which became known to Granda as 'the year Charlie Tully called' as opposed to 'the year McCormack sang in the house in Antrim' – I noticed drawings and sketches of my father's lying about the house. They were of players in Celtic hoops in the act of kicking or heading a ball. Their bodies were tiny but their heads were made from oval photos of the real players.

It was many years later – half a century, in fact – before I would remember these drawings again. My father died when I was twelve and my mother was so distraught that she threw out all his things. If she was reminded of him she would break down and weep so every scrap of paper relating to him had to be sacrificed.

Recently I was in Belfast and I wondered if there might be a copy of the programme lying around Smithfield market. I found a small shop entirely devoted to football programmes so I went in and told them what I was looking for – a Belfast Celtic v Glasgow Celtic Match programme from the early 50's.

The man looked at me and said,

'Put it this way. I'm a collector and I've never seen one.'

I was disappointed. Then he said,

'If you do catch up with it, you'll pay for it.'

'How much?' I was thinking in terms of twenty or thirty quid.

'A thousand pounds. Minimum.'

I'm not really impressed by that kind of rarity value – but in this case I thought, 'Good on you, Johnny. After all the work for charity.' If that price is accurate I don't want to own the real thing – but I wouldn't mind seeing a photocopy. A photocopy would be good. Above rubies, in fact.

a deep muffled

wo

noise

p22

NDED

from AROUND

the ground

The Match

Linda Cracknell

He stands with
his feet wide apart.
'I'm the goal.
You shoot.'

'Why you travel alone?' the guy who runs the guest house asks. He sits down opposite me, as he has taken to doing after serving the evening meals, and up-ends the box of dominoes so that the pieces clatter across the table. I've told him several times already that I don't play. Sometimes I watch for a while as he gets a group of four together. I get hypnotised by the fast slam of pieces as excitement grows, the flicker of dark looks that cross the table diagonally, the curl of a lip that leads them all into laughter. It's hard to see why they find it so much fun. I usually get bored after a while and retreat from the veranda, go down the stairs and cross the night-cool sand to my cabin.

As he poses the question about me being alone, he rolls one of his dreadlocks between thumb and forefinger. The thick strands spring stiff and prickly above his forehead before separating over his neck and shoulders. They look like dark wool that's been felted by the weather, bleached at the ends. He presses and twiddles at it like a child might do with a lock of hair when they're watching TV or concentrating on something. His head's on one side, his tired eyes looking over my shoulder out towards the dark smash of waves. His domino pals haven't appeared tonight.

I shrug. I suppose I have to answer him, though of course I'm not going to tell him the real reason I'm alone.

'I'm just here to chill out,' I say, then hear my stupid words. The damp evening air wraps my shoulders like a heavy cardigan. I'm hardly going to get chilly here. 'I mean relax. I'm here to relax. I don't need too much action.'

'You are relaxed now,' he says so that I can't tell if it's a question or a statement. He looks at me with a small grin, head cocked. 'You walk very fast when you first come.' He nods in the direction of the village and mimics scribbling with his hand. 'Very busy, writing postcards.'

I toy with one of the dominoes that has landed in front of me. It's smooth and cool to the touch. I close my fingers around it. When I first arrived I stayed out of the public places – the veranda, the beach. I only went to the village to send Kenneth's postcards. I walked fast to rebuff the invitations that seemed to emanate from the groups of people under trees – heat-basking, laughing, working at unexplained things with their hands. Two men hunched over a big wooden board, played a game in which they shifted collections of tiny shells across a series of bowls carved into it. It was as if they were crouched with marbles or Pokemon cards in a school playground. But I only glimpsed them from the corner of my eye at first.

They don't hide their own fascination. The kids in the village run after me, want to stroke my straight blonde hair and pinch at my white skin. The way adults stop and study me isn't much different. I let my curiosity wander a little more too. He's right. I have relaxed.

'And tomorrow,' he says. 'Is your last day. Is a pity.'

I feel sick. Maybe a reaction. Something in the supper. Or something in the question, forcing me back to the gut-twisting mess Kenneth's made of our holiday together.

'Look at that, Kenneth,' I had pointed at a photo in the guide book. I was sitting next to him, grazing my fingers against the soft-coarse brush up the back of his head where the hairdresser had sheared him. In the photo, the sky-blue upper and turquoise lower were divided by a strip of white sand on which a dhow was landing. Its huge white sail cut a diagonal across the middle of the photo. It promised beauty and adventure and excitement. Kenneth squinted at the men in the water who were pushing the boat ashore, wearing straw hats and torn T-shirts.

'It looks kind of basic there.' A stray thought panicked his face out of the guide book. 'Will there be TV? There might not even be TV.'

'There'll be so much else to do, Kenneth, you won't even miss it.' I laughed, nudging his reaction aside. After all, I had more or less persuaded him to go. I pictured us turning golden together, eating breakfasts of tropical fruit. Not being in a proper resort meant we wouldn't be hemmed in with other tourists. I'd have his undivided attention. He'd make me laugh like he did when we first met. Having a holiday together would cement things, make the future as clear as that turquoise water.

Lunch on my last day is kingfish and rice. As he lays the plate on the table in front of me, he flicks his head and scatters trails of hair, so they bounce soft against the skin of his face. It's like a mane. I can't help watching.

'What will you do. For your last afternoon?' he asks.

'The usual I guess.'

My curiosity strays in the sea breeze that blows through the upstairs veranda. Would it tickle or feel coarse – his hair? What would it be like to make love to someone with dreadlocks? Like the mating of lions – ferocious and soft at the same time?

I could tell Kenneth about this little fantasy when I get home. It might amuse him. I can almost hear him mutter.

'Larsson. Was it bloody Larsson you were dreaming of? Trust you to fraternise with the enemy. What are you playing at?'

And I wonder how on earth the picture of Larsson got into my head – the Celtic strip, and the swing of blond, Swedish dreadlocks. It's as if I've been brain-washed in my sleep.

I lie outside my cabin, in the shade, pouring along the hammock like an Arabian princess, belly rounded with rice and fish, toe trailing. All my books are finished and stacked up inside. I can occupy myself with indolence. Lying with the beach wind licking at my skin, I listen to the palm leaves rubbing and rustling against each other. Everyone else is resting after lunch. Dogs are dark flat shadows on the sand. There's a flash of reflected sun from way down the low-tide bleached runway of the beach, away from the safety of palm shade. A bicycle passing, sizzling in the heat on the white hard sand. Someone with an urgent crayfish delivery to a hotel, perhaps.

I buy a young coconut from the boy who comes each day with a bulging canvas bag. He slices a small lid off the top of the coconut and watches for a while, sitting in the sand as I drink the cool water from it. Afterwards he takes it back from me, slices the hole bigger with his huge grey knife and fashions a spoon from the spare husk. I know now what I'm supposed to do with it. I scoop out the soft white young flesh inside and let it slide sweet down my throat, barely chewing.

The boy huddles over three papayas and the glossy conch shell his mother has sent him out with. He shakes his head over them and every so often looks up at me. There aren't many other tourists here to sell things to. I've seen him in the evenings at the village playing-field, freed from his marketing duties, running and leaping barefoot with the other boys, all straining to make contact with a bundle of cloth tied into a ball with string. And if I close my eyes, it could be the kids on the green at home. The cries collide with each other and ring with the same urgency and outrage and joy. The punch and bounce of a proper ball are missing, but the language is universal.

In the days before I left home, a white sheet of snow came down onto the green. It wrapped streets and cars and buildings. An easterly wind was spraying it into drifts as I pored over the small print of the travel insurance, and news came in that our ice maidens over in Canada had struck gold.

'The housework Olympics,' Kenneth said to my TV. 'All that sweeping up. Scotland's females excel at that, eh?' He peered at the hawk's-hood of concentration on Rhona Martin's face as she sent the flat stone scudding across the ice. 'They look like plumbers' wives,' he said and turned to another channel.

Despite their victory, the girls still got pushed from the sports pages by pictures of footballers' muddy thighs. Somehow their ordinary names couldn't compete with the ones Kenneth recites, like Amoruso, Caniggia, Lovenkrands. I've never listened, but their names have taken hold somehow. They make me think of exotic desserts, full of cream and liqueur.

'You can't change the dates,' I told Kenneth. 'Death, illness, injury, bereavement, redundancy or jury service. We'll just have to lose the booking money. Or go.'

The heat's bearable now as I meander barefoot back on the firm shore, out in the open where the breeze fans and cools me. I haven't been all the way to the village. There's no point in sending postcards now, and anyway I've stopped thinking of things to tell him.

Because it's the east coast, the wind-lain palm trees are shading the beach, the squat, thatched houses hiding between them. The trunks of a few trees standing alone are filament-thin, cut by sunlight from behind. One of them, a crazy hieroglyphic, is a signpost for me.

The trunk of the twisted palm outside my guest house.

I see the figure on the beach from quite a distance. As I close in, I can see that he is naked except for shorts – the uniform of late afternoon recreation. For men, anyway. The figure is dancing on the spot. The feet point down, knees rise towards the chest one at a time, arms wing-like at the sides. It's balletic. It's as if the figure's on a vertical spring, bouncing rhythmically, perfectly balanced. But it's not until I'm quite close that I see the ball that's part of the dance too. He rolls it back and forwards on the sand, under each foot, then hooks a toe under it to flick it into the air. It rebounds from a raised knee; the chest pushes out to butt at it; the figure pirouettes to catch the bounce against his lower back.

The features refine as I get nearer the twisted palm. A bump of something on top of the head – dreadlocks tied into a knot, their ends flopping onto the back of the neck. The rounded muscle on arm and thigh and chest. Full lips, dark eyes, nostrils flared in concentration.

'Why do you play alone?' I ask when I get close enough for him to notice me.

He stops the ball in his hands and shrugs.

'You can play too,' he says, and drops the ball onto the ground.

'No, no, I can't. I don't.' I turn for my cabin.

'Is easy. Look.' He kicks the ball towards me. 'You're the goal first, then me.'

I don't understand. How can I be a goal?

'Like this.' He stands with his feet wide apart. 'I'm the goal. You shoot.'

The ball has rolled to a stop in front of me, hard to ignore, teasing me to attack it. With his feet apart he seems to have dropped in height, so we are eye to eye. He nods. I take a step back and gather my breath and concentration, my bare foot and poor vulnerable toes. I kick it, straight between his feet. Clean. A clear-cut goal. A rush of something bounds me up and down.

'I've never done that before.'

'Now my turn,' he says. 'The first one to three goals is the winner. If I win, you have to make a presentation to me. If you win, I make to you. OK?'

'Present what?'

'The presenter chooses.'

'OK,' I hesitate while I mentally rifle my luggage for something I don't need which would make a suitable gift. The first thing I think of is a comb, a nice turquoise one. Then I look at his head and remember. Of course, he doesn't use a comb.

He dribbles the ball along the beach, the knot of his hair bouncing. I grin, but his eyes grip the space between my feet. He kicks hard and the ball bumps my foot, bounces away from the goal. I grab it.

'My turn,' I say, scenting victory. I picture myself holding the shiny cup handles, the roar of the stadium pushing the trophy up above my head. Would Kenneth believe that I actually *played* football? And *enjoyed* it.

'But what will you do?' Kenneth had glared at me when I said I'd go on my own. I only said it to get a reaction. I really couldn't imagine what anyone would do on holiday on their own. But it might just make him change his mind if I called his bluff.

'I mean,' he'd said. 'You're not really going to find a table-tennis club in a place like that. Are you?'

'I'll take a pile of books. I'm not a child you know – I don't need games. I just need a holiday.' Saying it almost made me believe it.

'But you're hardly a lone ranger, pal.'

'Come with me then.'

He tipped his head on the one side, creased his eyes like he was dead sad about it. 'You know I can't, love.' He took my hands, swallowed hard like he was going to tell me someone had died or something. 'I know you're not a big fan of the game. It's hard for you to understand, but... You do know this match could mean the quarter finals, don't you?'

Those turquoise waters froze into a lump in my throat. And then I knew I'd have to see the bluff through. I went upstairs right then and opened a suitcase on the bedroom floor. I dropped things into it as I thought of them, when I passed it over the next few days.

When I left my flat for the airport, I noticed the black tarmac rectangle that Kenneth's car had cut into the snow, where he'd been parked. His car had been there a lot in recent weeks. And now it was marking out his territory even when he wasn't there. But then, it was starting to snow again.

I look at my watch by the candlelight that the wind flickers across the supper table, and calculate the hours across the oceans. The match will be about to start now. Somehow I know the kick-off time. How sad. The pub will be bubbling with testosterone, wall to wall with blue nylon, Kenneth at the centre of it. They'll be gripping pints at the bar, repeating the ritual stories, 'Mind that time when Beanie...?' And after the laughter's bent them double, they'll practise the usual jokes. There's the one about not swerving to hit a cyclist who's a Celtic fan. Because it's probably your bicycle. And something about Celtic fans and dole queues. I'm always careful not to take the bait but I suspect he laughs a lot louder when I'm not about.

After the evening meals have finished, and the other diners have left the veranda for their cabins, he beckons me to join him behind the bar. He gives me a stool to sit on. This is new. Not joining me at the table. No dominoes. The breeze from the night sea has swelled up so much that my skin almost puckers into goose-bumps. He pours a glass of something creamy coloured.

'What is it?' I ask.

He pushes the bottle towards me and points at the label. I have to peer closely because it's gloomy behind the bar. There's an elephant and some round yellow fruit.

'This tree, wild marula. They call it the "elephant tree".' He puts the glass in front of me. 'This is your prize. For winning the football match.'

'Thank you. A grand prize,' I say, still glowing from my victory.

He lays a hand over mine as I reach to take the glass. 'But there's a special way to drink it. A game.' He picks up the glass, its contents luminously pale against his small, pointed fingers. 'You take a drink, then pass it to me.'

It takes me a moment to get what he means, to realise that I somehow already know the rules of this game. I open my mouth for him. He pours sweet cream onto my tongue and I hold it there while eye burns on eye and his teeth glint in a soft smirk, waiting. I circle the drink in my mouth. It tastes smooth and strokes the bare skin of my neck and arms back to warmth. Then I'm slipping towards him from my stool, and pouring from my mouth into his, slippery with fruit and cream, drinking.

We are the same height. Knee to knee, chin to chin, each limb fits the other. I feel the graze of tendrils sprinkling against my face. His hand silks at my hair.

No-one's watching. Eyes at home will be fixed on a Dutch stadium. I'm part of the game now, as a player, not a spectator. My hands are on the back of his head, closing soft on dreadlocks, stroking his mane.

This Is My Story, This Is My Song

Laura Hird

When victory
finally arrived,
it was like we didn't
know the words.

'...He was meant to meet us at the snooker club. We were waiting in the bar when I got the call. The cunt doing sixty in the Range Rover landed in a field with whiplash and a dislocated wrist. He phoned the ambulance. His mobile was still fucking working, can you believe that? Ronnie's van spun over three times then smashed face down on a wall. He had no chance.'

I read Ian's e-mail for about the tenth time, but still it seems like a newspaper story you'd see about some stranger.

The driving was Ronnie's first real work since the engineering plant burnt down, taking with it his job, pension and savings he'd been encouraged to invest in the company's shares. I try to work out where Granton and the shell of the plant should be, as my plane drops over the Forth. The surge of pride I always feel when I fly over the Bridges overtakes me though. I think its called coming home.

I grab a taxi rather than wait ten minutes for the airport bus. It's already half-nine and we're leaving for Mortonhall about eleven. They'll all have been in the pub since it opened. Not that I want to get pissed. I just need a few swifties to help me deal with the fact that Ronnie won't be there. Not today, not ever.

By Ingliston, I'm getting really maudlin, thinking about the last time I spoke to him. He phoned about hospitality tickets for the Hearts/Celtic game I couldn't make it up for. I said they must have got lost in the post. They're still sitting on top of my fridge. I just never bothered my arse.

I phone Steph on the mobile to cheer myself up. She's on her way out to Chalk Farm to buy more useless shite to clutter our flat. She's snappy because she hates me coming up for the home games, and thinks my best pal's funeral is some added sort of drunken conspiracy.

'So why didn't you phone me last time you were there? Why switch your mobile off?'

I get this one every couple of days. It's a cardinal sin. Thirty-six hours a month, I come up here, go see the football, kick a ball about for two hours, then fly down again. She tells me not to bother coming back. This time it's really over. As I'm already in Russell Road, this sounds fine so I hang up, and switch off the phone.

Ian's outside the pub, as we pull up. He's gabbing into his mobile, swaggering about, dead cocky, doesn't notice me paying the driver. I slam the taxi door.

'Hey cunt, want some?'

He turns around with his magic big grin.

'Christ, I know you're a thespian but d'you have to dress like one of The Persuaders for fucksake?'

Maybe the black polo neck was a bad idea. He gestures to his mobile then the pub and grabs his crotch. I can guess who's on the other end.

Soon as I walk in, I know I'm right. Colin and his wife, Karen, are at the end of the bar. She's giggling into her mobile, with a naughty, nasty look on her face. Surely Colin realises? It's been years now. They used to pay Ronnie to sit down here so they could use his flat. Ian works at the bank along the road but stays in Livingston.

It was a dead convenient arrangement.

Colin's over with my pint before I realise he's noticed me. He greets me with one of his crap jokes.

'How d'you get dandruff off a cunt?'

I say I don't know, he brushes my shoulder and hoots with laughter.

'Christ Col, I've not heard that one since primary.'

'You always say that.'

He tells me the arrangements, somehow managing to avoid saying Ronnie's name. It's just turned ten but the pub's packed. The jukebox is going full whack but it's still barely audible over the boom of conversation. The posties are already half cut, inventing songs of their own. Old George is shovelling coal onto the fire, which he then sits in front of, hogging the heat. Stewart the steward's at the jukebox, trying to get June to dance. She's threatening to punch his lights out. Most of the West End Hearts are in. Just like any Saturday morning I've flown up to go to the game with Ronnie, aside from a few bad suits and the absence of Ronnie.

My first pint doesn't last five minutes. Ian's still outside. Karen's still on her mobile. Colin, still oblivious, pulls a deranged face at Frankie, who's gone self-destructive on the puggie and hasn't even noticed me. I buy a round and take him over a pint of cider. He stares through me.

'Christ man, I thought I was doing him a favour, getting him that job.'

I stick the glass in his hand to stop him shovelling more money into the machine.

'He was just chuffed to be working again, Frankie. You gave him that, Christ.'

He downs half his pint and looks very serious.

'Know what they're saying now, eh? He hadnae driven in years. I've got him fannying about the central belt in a Bedford, for fucksake. I should've checked it out, Ken. It's down to me, it really is.'

Sorry as I feel for him, I'm already looking round for Colin to rescue me. He's gone to phone his son, Paul, to see if he's coming. Paul's in the Hearts Juniors what Ronnie was helping out with while he studied for his SFA licences.

The barmaid's on the phone though, and Colin's been hi-jacked by singing posties. I try to sidetrack Frankie by asking about work. Frankie loves boasting about how well he's doing. He tells me about some tenement he's doing up in Pilrig, and the great crew that's working for him, the IKEA kitchens some guy from the snooker club's sneaking out for two hundred pound a piece. Then he's back on a downer. Ronnie'd picked up some flat-packs just prior to the accident, apparently.

'I cannae handle it Ken, honestly. I know what they're all saying. I'd be saying the same.'

'Don't be daft. Christ, come on. We'll play five-a-side tomorrow. Beat the fucking Arabs up the Meadows. That's what Ronnie'd want.'

'But there's just four of us now.'

'So we'll get June in goals or something. Stop blaming yourself. Fuck.'

He knocks back his pint and says he'll get another while I catch up. He's obviously decided to deal with this the way he deals with everything – rat-arsed. Maggie, the manageress only notices I'm in when she comes back with his change. She lets out a shriek, and comes running round to see me.

'Aw Kenneth, how's my favourite actor?'

I don't get time to answer.

'Did you hear about Ronnie's family? The roll shop's done food. The brewery gave a few bottles for nips. But no, we're no good enough, sweetheart. Too common.'

She shakes her head and gives me her I-don't-even-want-to-go-there look. Aw, she's a Hibbie but she's brilliant.

'So what is happening afterwards? I'm not going with his lot. I'll end up in Saughton.'

'Just get as many of them back here as you can, sweetheart. The West End Hearts are coming back. This lot won't have moved. Show these snobby buggers who his real pals were.'

Thank God for that. This was Ronnie's pub. These radges were his real family. Maggie's probably glad of the extra business on a non-match day but her heart's in the right place, no pun intended. She shouts on the new barmaid to pass her fags.

'So how's the life of a Hollywood jetsetter? I watched your Rebus thing with the girls the other week. We were screaming at the telly.'

'I wasnae that bad, was I?'

She looks horrified.

'You were brilliant, sweetheart. Lauren took that photo of the pair of you to school next day to show off. Really. We watch the video when daddy's working.'

'I only had about three lines.'

'Aye, but they were great. You really showed that John Hannah up. C'mon though, what's your latest? When do I next have to set the video?'

Frankie looks pissed off and has already arsed his catch-up pint. He says he'll get us one while he's waiting. Maggie wants an answer though.

'Ocht, the usual rubbish. A Glaswegian junkie in The Bill – no dialogue. I just jump out a window when they knock my door down. Oh, and an alkie doctor in some Ruth Rendell thing. I rehearsed my two lines for that on the plane.'

'The plane! Oh Kenneth, what a life you lead. Aw, ma wee film star.'

Frankie shakes his head in disgust. Maggie scowls at him behind his back.

'Well before you disappear back to film land this time, I want an autograph. The girls too. They'll be worth a fortune one day.'

At least someone has a wee bit faith in me, misguided though it is.

Colin re-appears as Frankie hands me my pint.

'I'll have one too, ta.'

'Christsake. You must smell me getting my money out, man.'

'It's the moths, Frankie,' I laugh.

'Mammoths, more like,' mutters Col.

Ian finally comes in, as Karen puts her mobile in her bag. He shouts Frankie to get him a drink as he's handing Col his.

'Fucksake. What is it with youz and your timing?'

'Make it a double Morgan's then,' says Ian.

Frankie gets him a pint.

'You'll take what you're given, you blue-nose wanker.'

Colin grins at me and points to Karen.

'What about her, Frankie? She's sitting with a glass full of ice.'

'When I see her buy a round, I'll buy her one,' says Frankie.

Karen storms off to the Ladies. Within seconds, Ian's mobile goes off and he's back outside with his drink.

'Fucking liberty,' growls Frankie. 'He's only speaking to me when he wants bevy. See, every cunt does think it's my fault.'

Col's looking about, to see where Karen's got to. It's gone silent between Frankie and me. Luckily Ian's back in quickly.

'Sorry about that. Women, eh?' he winks. 'Anyway, good you managed to escape, Ken. Did you get shit as well? How is she? Nah, fuck women. How's acting?'

Colin starts singing the can't-get-quicker-than-a-Quickfit-fitter song, as he always does when my job's mentioned. Bastard. He'll never let me live down my first TV appearance. It re-ignites Frankie.

'Aye, you should have heard Maggie going on about wanting his autograph. It'll be worth a fortune if he ever does anything decent, apparently.'

Col's still singing the stupid jingle in my other ear. Ian, Rangers bastard that he is, at least defends me.

'You can laugh. I sent Lorraine through to Glasgow the other week.

George Best was signing his book. It's was seventeen quid but they're selling signed one's on the Internet for a hundred. She got me five, so I know who *will* be laughing when *he* pops his clogs.'

Frankie's reached the bottom of another glass.

'Get Ewan McGregor here to sign some beer-mats, then murder him. We'll all be minted.'

'Aye, well you've got the track record. We'll leave that up to you, eh, Frankie?'

I half-expect him to clock Ian one, but incredibly, he keeps on at me.

'Fuck you. And him – too busy playing smackie, wife-beating twat-heids to send Ronnie that ticket for his last Hearts game.'

I let it go. He's right. The realisation that Ronnie must have told them all about it, makes me feel like utter shite.

Ian tries to shut him up by getting another round. Frankie's been going on so much he still has a full pint, but accepts one anyway. Karen's up at the juke box, so Colin's trying to charm the new barmaid with his crap jokes. Who can blame him, considering?

'See when we get back, Julie, will you comfort me against your bosom?'

'Aye sure. I'll suffocate you,' she says, pulling pints without even looking up.

Billy, the grouchiest man on the planet, comes over to ask if we're going to the funeral. Like, we were only his best friends!

'Nah, we're auditioning for the St Bride's production of Reservoir Dogs.'

The dour bastard blanks me and says he's going with Duncan the drunken taxi driver. I have a fleeting fantasy about them crashing, then feel bad for thinking such a thing in the circumstances.

Ian points at his watch. The hearse is due outside the stadium in ten minutes. We all have drink left, but he buys us each a double, regardless. Frankie looks stunned. We make a toast to Ronnie then knock them back in one. It's shocking, really, driving pissed to the funeral of a best pal killed in a car crash. Ian's a careful driver, though. Even when he's off his face. And it's not like I can drive so I can hardly criticise.

It's after five-to when we leave. Lots of folk are already away. Even a few of the posties have gone with Stewart the steward and June. As we stumble out the back door, I suddenly think, wait, Ronnie must still be in the bogs. Then I remember.

The hearse and limo drive by as we come out the pub. I see Ronnie's horrible sister staring out disapprovingly, as it passes. Frankie's staggering about the place as well. Typical.

We pile into Ian's car but Frankie insists first on having a piss behind a van. Fucksake. We'll miss the minute's silence outside Tynecastle. He's twenty feet away, the engine's running but I can still hear it, gushing out the twat. He finally wobbles towards us, banging his head on the way in. Ian's seething.

'Christ Frankie, I know you're a Celtic supporter, but do you have to act like a fucking weedgie all the time?'

It's not until we turn into the street, I realise there's about two dozen folk standing outside the front of the pub. A sea of black, white and maroon. Mourners with scarfs; regulars; some of the West End crowd; the boys from the bookies; some parents from the juniors; the old morning crew; even a couple of radges from Stratties and the sports shop.

'This is my story,

this is my song,

Follow the Hearts and you can't go wrong...'

I get an instant lump in my throat.

'...Oh some say that Celtic and Rangers are grand

But the boys in maroon are the best in the land...'

'The fucking hairs are up on the back of my neck. And I hate the Jambo cunts,' says Ian.

Frankie's shaking his head, shiny-eyed.

'I'll waste that Range-Rover, Barbour-jacketed bastard. See when it comes to court. I'll take a fucking knife.'

'...H-E-A...R-T-S,

If you cannae spell it then here's what it says...'

Colin, the Hibbie, is just gawping at them.

'Christ, Ronnie'd fucking love this.'

By the time we get along to the stadium, the hearse, limo and a couple of other cars are already parked. No sooner have we stopped behind them, though, they take off. It's only just turned eleven. It's like they've seen us and changed their minds.

'Fuck it Ian, have our own minute's silence. There's plenty time, yet.'

He kills the engine and we synchronise watches. Its thirty seconds past eleven. I look across at Tynecastle, half-expecting Ronnie to knock on the window and ask us what the fuck we're doing. I'm getting choked up again, so I try to think of any old shite to get Ronnie and his brilliant laugh out my head but it's like trying to give up smoking. There suddenly doesn't seem to be anything else to think about.

When Frankie's mobile goes off, with about fifteen seconds to go, I'm sort of relieved. Fields of fucking Athenry though. What a twat. He fumbles to switch it off.

As soon as the minute's up, Ian leans over and grabs him by the ear.

'Just make sure it's off during the service, or I'll break your fucking neck.'

For once, Frankie seems genuinely embarrassed.

'Like I'm that ignorant, Ian, eh? Gimme a break.'

As we drive towards Mortonhall, it goes quiet in the car. Like we're afraid to speak in case it sparks off another argument. It reminds me of the weird, stunned silence on the bus back from the '98 Cup Final. I was there with Ronnie. After thirty-five years supporting Hearts, when victory finally arrived, it was like we didn't know the words. It struck us temporarily dumb. I stare out the window at a passing Edinburgh that'll never quite be the same again. The streets seemed strangely hushed. Even the roads are quiet. Unsurprisingly, it's Frankie that breaks the silence.

'Put some fucking sounds on, eh? This no speaking's doing my head in.'

For once he goes unchallenged. I think we're all starting to feel the same. The radio gets switched on just in time to hear Meatloaf screech the immortal line,

'...now I'm dying at the bottom of a pit in the blazing sun...'

'Brilliant,' mutters Ian, quickly changing stations. *'Everybody Hurts'* is next up. We groan in unison. I usually love that song but not today. And certainly not *'Stan,'* which is Forth FM's offering. Ian gives up and sticks on one of the dance music stations. We all hate dance music, but at least it doesn't make me think anything other than what the fuck is that?

By the time we get to the crematorium, the coffin and congregation are already inside. The undertakers are about to close the doors and come out for a fag. Ian double parks and we speed-walk down the path, past a row of floral tributes.

'Christ, did anyone get a wreath?'

Ian shrugs. 'Like he cares now.'

Colin agrees. 'Aye, fuck that. We'll do what we arranged. That'll be fine.'

'Aye, whap those fucking Arabs tomorrow,' grunts Frankie, 'Here, hang on, I need another piss.'

Ian yanks him by the arm.

'Just fucking move it. It'll only last ten minutes. They've got the next one to fry at quarter to twelve.'

The doors are closed behind us. It's in the smallest crematorium, so there's already half the Hearts bus standing at the back. I don't want to see the curtains at the side of the coffin tremble as it goes down anyway. It always makes me want to laugh, for some horrible reason. I can't see his family from here either, which suits me fine.

The female minister gives a wee spiel about Ronnie that she probably does a dozen times a day. As none of us were asked, it's all about family, work, morality and perseverance. She makes him sound like a fucking Mormon.

She makes us pray and then mime along to a hymn that no-one seems to know. There aren't any hymn books at the back, which makes it even more ridiculous. What's all this crap got to do with Ronnie anyway? They should play some Rod Stewart or Stevie Wonder. We should be singing a Hearts song. Something he liked, surely? Ronnie didn't even believe in God. Who does these days apart from Anne Widdecombe and Sir Cliff?

We're forced into a final prayer, before the organ starts up, the doors are opened and it's over. You're supposed to wait for the family to leave first, but we can't get out of there quick enough. There's too many at the back for all that ceremonious shit. No danger of that anyway as Frankie's straight behind a tree.

'I don't believe that bastard,' mutters Col.

A group of kids spot him, and start laughing and pointing. Luckily Ian misses this as he's back on his mobile. Jesus, does he never give his dick a day-off? Ronnie's family are too busy giving funny handshakes at the chapel door to even notice we're here. I stand well back to keep it that way.

Colin's laddie, Paul's here with the rest of the Hearts juniors. He's a Hibbie, like Col, but at least he plays for the right team. Col's trying to get him to come with us but he's got a training session this afternoon.

'It's the first one without Ronnie, dad. I sort of want to be there.'

Col squeezes his shoulder.

'Aye, you're right. Good laddie.'

I feel a stab of pride for the boy and a sadness that Ronnie never had any kids. Then Frankie's back over doing up his zip.

'So what's it like playing for the enemy, Paul? Never tempted to do a bit of a Bruce Grobbelar?'

I have to hold Colin back.

'What do your kids do like, Frankie? You don't even fucking know, do you, so shut the fuck up.'

Now Frankie's going for Colin. Ian swats him away with his mobile.

'Christ, have a bit of respect, the pair of you, eh? They already think we're scumbags. Dinnae confirm it, fucksake.'

Too late. Over his shoulder I see Ronnie's cunt of a sister heading our way. She's dabbing away tears, but has an expression of false sincerity that would make Neil Hamilton blush.

'She must have an onion in her bag,' I mumble as she walks up to Ian.

'I just wanted to thank you all for coming. We didn't expect many people, so we appreciate you making the effort.'

What's she on about? It was like an Edinburgh Derby in that crematorium. Patronising bitch.

'Best turn-out I've ever seen,' says Colin. 'Ronnie had lots of good friends. My laddie's in the juniors he worked with.

They're all here as well.'

Without acknowledging him, she says there's a buffet for twenty booked at the Orwell, so there's only room for family and close friends.

'As I said, though, thank you all for coming anyway.'

I see Frankie snarling. Ian pushes in front of him.

'That's fine. There's a big function at the pub for everybody.'

'How appropriate. I suppose they'll need all the business they can get, now Ronnie's gone.'

The tears are gone. And so, thank fuck, is she. Again, I seek solace in brief, inappropriate car crash fantasies.

'Surely Ronnie must've been swapped at birth,' Colin speculates.

Frankie agrees. 'We should've just stayed in the pub. That was a fucking farce. Hear her going on about Ronnie like he was some kind of alkie. Ugly auld trout.'

It seems like a good time to leave. We tell a few folk we'll see them back at the pub, then get in the car.

'D'you think that bitch'll get the flat? Fuck, just the thought of her nosing through the place and chucking half his things out. That can't be right, surely?'

I know Ian still has keys for Ronnie's place. I wonder if he means we should salvage some personal stuff before she gets her claws in. On second thoughts, he's probably more worried that his love-nest is about to go down the plughole. I wouldn't be surprised if Karen and him were at it up there before Ronnie was even cold.

'Thank fuck that Tanya left him before he had time to marry her. She'd probably turn it into a knocking shop,' says Col.

God, I'd forgotten about Tanya. Another of Ian's conquests. I notice his shoulders stiffening up when she's mentioned. Thank fuck Ronnie never found out.

We drive back through the wooded path from the crematorium then turn right, out of town. Frankie's confused.

'What are you playing at? Fuck the scenic route, I'm gasping on a pint.'

I assumed he'd been told about the arrangement.

'Just shut it, eh? It won't take long,' says Ian, turning onto the bypass.

We pass a sign for Hillend. Frankie seems to click and slumps back down in his seat. We're there in a couple of minutes.

It seems to appear out of nowhere, even though I'm expecting it. The right side of Lothianburn junction is scattered with flowers, rosettes and scarfs. I feel sick and sad and proud, all at once. As Ian parks on a grass verge behind the junction, a horrible sense that we shouldn't be here starts to grip me. But the rest of them get out, so I have to follow. I don't want to have to try and explain.

We cross over to what's left of the fence. I feel weak and shell-shocked, as if I've just stepped out of a car crash. Even the police cordon has cards, match tickets, Hearts key-rings hung on it. The grass is black, oily and charred though and there's pieces of twisted metal and broken glass everywhere. Every time a car goes past on the by-pass, it makes me shudder. This is horrible. I want away from here.

When Ian produces a half bottle of Grouse and paper cups from a carrier bag, my instinct is to start running.

'We'll have this and then go,' he whispers, handing us each an equal dram.

I take mine over to what's left of the fence. I just want to be on my own until this is over. Lighting a fag is a bad move though. They're all over, wanting one. Ian and Colin don't even smoke.

Thankfully, Ian takes his and goes to sit in the car.

Frankie goes wandering off down the road to deal with his own demons.

Colin crosses over to the other side of the junction and sits with his back to us, facing the black hulk of the Pentlands.

I slug back some whisky, close my eyes and try to block the present out. Try to let my mind take me to some happier time, with Ronnie. The Ronnie I want to remember, on the bus home from the '98 Cup Final.

It was strangely subdued to begin with. Like we couldn't take in the fact that we'd actually won. It wasn't till we reached the outskirts of Edinburgh that realisation started to sink in and excitement break out, like a rash. The singing started up. First just a few of us, unfamiliar with our new song,

'We won the cup, we won the cup...'

By Sighthill, they started coming out onto the streets. An old woman with a zimmer, maroon-clad kids on their father's shoulders, old boys waving flags out of windows, gangs of bairns, draped in banners.

'We won the cup, we won the cup...'

Pubs and shops emptying onto the road to welcome us back to Gorgie. The great, big noise of hooters, cheering, chanting, car horns, drums. The bus shuddering as we stomp our way home, singing and sobbing and hoping the fuck it wasn't just a dream.

'WE WON THE CUP, WE WON THE CUP...'

Ian starts blaring the horn.

'C'mon, we better be making a move.'

I wait till the tears stop, then stand up and raise my cup to the sky; to the Jambos; to Ronnie.

Football Scarves and Richard Kimble

Iain Maloney

an enormous snake
of green, white and
gold weaving its way
through the streets

He wound down the window and pulled in the green and white scarf that hung limp, the wind having died. He carefully placed it round his neck making sure that it didn't cover the logo or the CR SMITH banner across the front of his shirt.

– C'mon then, we've a wee walk ahead of us.

He was tensing up to slam the door, making sure this time, when he noticed them. The army. Marching. An enormous snake of green, white and gold weaving its way through the streets. He'd never seen so many people before, they were everywhere he looked, taking over the city.

– Grand innit?

He'd seen this on TV, the crowds, but it was so much bigger. The cameras showing them limited within certain areas, defined by the curve of the stands. This was his first. See it live. Feel the atmosphere. Watch them spilling like liquid into every space. Jock Stein end. Celtic end. Hampden. Magic words. Centenary year. Centenary meant 100. 1888 – 1988. He was eight. That made Celtic 92 years older than him. Older than Grandad.

– Jist like it wis in the 60's. Nine in a row. A tell yi a wis at the games? All o them. Afore an eifter an all. Charlie drove the bus in '67. Year we won the European Cup. First British team, first Catholic.

– Billy McNeil was in it wasn't he dad?

– Sure was. Great man. Gony get us the double this year. Dundee United? Who are they anyway? Orange bastards, scuse my French.

Trying to avoid the muddy puddles so as to keep his socks white he fell in line behind his dad, his colours matching perfectly with the rest. He could hear singing but couldn't understand most of it.

– Hullo, hullo...

– Oh it's a grand old team tae play fur...

– Hail Hail...

A big man with a beard was beside him. He had a boy with him in an away strip. He'd wanted one as well but it cost too much for both.

– Better tae have to hoops though eh?

Still it looked cool.

– Orite bigman? First game?

– Aye.

The beard looked above his head, over at his dad.

– Good choice for a first time eh but?

– Aye, centenary and a possible double.

– Nae possible aboot it, in the bag. Naebdy in orange's gony stand in the way of the Celtic.

– Aye.

The beard was separated from them as the crowd moved on.

– A mind when a wis ur age, mibbe a bit younger, the bus takin thi Rangers fans tae Hampden aywis passed the end o our street in Brigton. Wan day me an ma mate went oot in oor full altar boy gear when the bus wis stopped at the lights. We nealt doon on the pavement an blessed the bus.

He laughed as he made a cross in the air.

– They startid bangin on the windaes an then we hears the door openin so wi pegged it. Got chased in an oot o aw the closes. Got skelped by Kit fur makin such a mess a me guid clathes.

He tried to imagine doing that himself. Kneeling in front of Rangers fans, intimidating them like that. It didn't make sense though. How do you bless a bus? Apart from making the sign of the cross in the air what else happened? He was still worrying about this when they turned a corner and there it was up ahead. Hampden.

– That's Scotland's ground innit dad?

– Aye and Queens Park.

This made no sense.

– How can two teams use the same ground?

– Well Scotland dinnae play that many games so Queens Park use it the rest o the time.

– What happens when they both have to play on the same day?

– Never happens.

– But...

– Never happens.

Confused he looked around at the other fans. All so happy. It made him feel happy, welcomed. We are the people. He wasn't though. His dad had told him that. A choochter. Not from Glasgow.

– Still, could have been worse. Could be a Hun, from Govan or somethin.

He was from Aberdeen. Sheep-shaggers. He didn't know what that meant but knew it was bad and not to be said in front of his parents. His friends all supported Aberdeen. He didn't. Kept getting beaten up for it.

– Who's better?

– Celtic.

Wallop.

– Who's better?

– Celtic.

Wallop.

– Who's better?

– We thrashed ye four-nil. Sheep-shagger.

Wallop.

He just didn't see the attraction. Red wasn't a good colour. Green and white was. Plus they kept getting beat. Or drawing. Nil-Nil. Where's the excitement I that? There was a sneaking suspicion that he should really support his local team but he just got so bored watching them. Couldn't get worked up like with Celtic.

– Can I have a programme dad?

– Sure, souvenir.

They moved through the crowd until they were at the stand.

– A programme please pal.

– Sure. His first time?

– Aye.

– Guid day fur it.

– Aye. Glorious.

– Golden sun. Just need a green and white sky.

– Dad, can I have that scarf.

– Yiv got a scarf.

– But look at that wan.

It was amazing. It said CELTIC F.C. in huge white letters down the middle. Above this it said "League Champions 1987-88" and below it said "Scottish Cup Winners 1988". In the bag.

– Yiv got wan.

– But Dad...

– No.

– Look, if it his first game al gie ye it fur two fifty.

– Go on Dad.

– Okay. And dinnae say a niver dae anythin fur ye.

His Dad took the first scarf, put it on and looked at his watch.

– Better get a move on.

– What time is it?

– Quarter to. Fifteen minutes. Did I tell ye about wan game a wis at? Y'know The Fugitive.

– No.

– It wis a programme that wis on years ago. About this guy Doctor Richard Kimble. His wife had been murdered and it wis made to look like he did it.

– Did he?

– No but he wis arrested then escaped. He knew that a wan armed man hid dun it an the whole series wis based round him tryin to find the wan armed man without getting caught. Onyway the last episode wis on at the same time as this game. Wednesday night. Abdy watched The Fugitive but there are mair important things than TV so we went tae the game. Me and Charlie.

– Why d'you call Grandad Charlie?

– That's his name. A dinnae like callin him Dad.

– Why?

– Niver you mind. So we're at the game an it gets tae half time and we've got oor pies an Bovril an everywans either talkin aboot the game or aboot The Fugitive.

– What wis the score?

– Cannae mind. Onyway the guy comes on the tannoy...

– Whits that?

– The loudspeaker that they use to tell abdy whits happening.

– Like the commentary on TV?

– No, jist things like substitutions. So this guy comes on the tannoy and announces that they've found the wan armed man and this huge cheer goes up round the stand. Made abdys night.

They were at the stadium. There were even more people here than on the street. It seemed impossible. The whole world must be here.

– Right, stay close.

Before he realised it they were entering the stand. Celtic end. He looked in front of himself and saw the pitch. Beautiful green. Dark and light stripes like on TV. He saw the goals, where the action would happen. Then he saw the rest of the stadium. So many people. Green and white spilled out in front of him, stopping abruptly when the orange and black began round the other end. The Rangers end Dad called it. It was unbelievable. He felt himself sinking, lost in amongst all the colour. He noticed a huge Irish flag travelling across the top of the Celtic fans. He had a Scotland flag at home on the back of his door. He imagined himself passing the flag across the fans and then felt a sickness as he realised he would never get it back, would lose his Saltire forever. He felt sorry for whoever's flag it was. He heard a shout and realised he couldn't move forwards. Looking down he saw a metal bar across his chest. Turnstile. He turned and saw his Dad right behind him, a comforting presence.

– Calm down tae fuck. Jist a kid. First fuckin time. Here ye go.

His Dad handed over the magical tickets, the ones that had come a month ago through the post. They'd been waiting when he came home from school. Big pieces of paper, a dotted line half way along. Celtic v. Dundee United in huge letter across the front, loads of small writing on the back.

– On you go then.

He felt a hand on his back and stumbled forwards, the turnstile moving around him. A ticket stub was pushed into his hand. He held it close to him, afraid to lose it as a huge cheer went up.

A shiver ran down his back.

First fuckin time.

The Hand of God Squad

Gordon Legge

Flo said, 'You okay?'
'Yeah. I've just found out
I'm adopted.
My real dad's Kevin Keegan.'

You forget sometimes that half our pubs, the ones we grew up with, are actually hotels: The Abbey, The Queens and The Orchard; The Belford, The Belvedere and The Grange. I suppose, by way of excuse, you could blame the teenage beer blinkers. We slouched off and we seen what we what we wanted to see – a side entrance and its public bar.

Me and Noxie discovered our drinking heads round at The Belford. Soon as we were of age, and earning, we'd be out three of the four nights: depending on whether Question Time was on or not, either the Thursday through the Saturday, or the Friday through the Sunday. The Belford was never busy, its clientele a handful of nicey nice central belt, middle income couples. Or, as Noxie put it: the dull, thick and married, the dull, thick and engaged, and the dull, thick and going steady. Me and Noxie had our seats through the back and down the stairs, in the conservatory. Apart from ourselves, nobody much bothered with the conservatory, granting us the perfect peace to practice our drinking and go on about the things we went on about – telly, books, the news and our travelling. Me and Noxie talked all the time. During the week, something daft on the telly and we'd be phoning each other to talk about it. The same things would tickle us.

We only ever spent a couple of hours down the pub. After, we'd sometimes get a takeaway. Noxie, being the bigger earner, always treated. At the junction of Inchyra and Wholeflats, Noxie was supposed to go his way, and I was supposed to go mine. Yet often, come daylight, we'd still be there, and still talking. Here, the conversation could get a bit candid. We'd mention girls we were hung up on at our respective works. We'd share confidences. We'd talk about the future. Sleepy-eyed and stifling yawns, we'd stand in silence, waiting for one or the other to start up a new thread.

It's a wonder we never got bored. We said it was cause we were never boring. More likely, we didn't know any better. Well, not at home, anyway.

A change was probably due. Trouble was, we were never going to instigate it. As luck would have it, we didn't have to. One night, we arrived at The Belford to discover a notice taped to the side entrance door. The public bar was closed for refit. It would be closed for a month. The management, bless them, apologised for any inconvenience. Best part of five years we'd been going there, and nobody'd thought to mention it. If this had happened in Denver, Paris or Gothenburg, or anywhere else, it wouldn't have been a problem. But here, our home, where we lived and worked, and always had, 'problem' didn't begin to tell the half of it. The Belvedere, The Queens and The Grange were all winner stays on at pool, zoomer city affairs. The Grange's toilet had chin high sinks. The Abbey, meanwhile, was geared up for the grey pound, and the zoomers with zimmers. They liked their themed nights down The Abbey, and they liked volume. If it wasn't a blaring Bontempi Bob, it would be a pair of boys with accordions. The nightly prize bingo could be heard three streets away.

As far as getting a drink went, that just left The Orchard. The Orchard was all sixth years and students. Me and Noxie hated sixth years and students. When it was through in Glasgow one time, me and Noxie made it onto the audience for Question Time. We'd to fill out these cards, with our names, occupations, and the questions we wanted to ask. Noxie's question was about how students – 'the fickle spawn of safety net rich mummies and daddies' – could be justified in getting such a thing as subsidised beer. Noxie's wasn't one of the questions chosen.

Me and Noxie left school at sixteen, end of fourth year. We told the careers wife, as long as it didn't involve slaving our guts out to make some rich cunt richer, we were happy doing anything. The careers wife suggested the public services. I got taken on at the infirmary, working with laundry. You name it, I was up to my elbows in it. Noxie got a start with the council, as a trainee housing officer. We were good with money, and, every month, starting with a hundred, put some away. Aside from the travelling, there was no extravagance. We lived with our folks. We didn't drive. We didn't smoke. We didn't own fifty pairs of trainers. Our weekly treat was just four quiet pints, two rounds each, three out of our four nights. It wasn't much to ask for.

I said to Noxie, 'Where d'you reckon we should go then?'

'Vilnius,' he said.

We'd a thing about Vilnius.

The bottom line was, we wanted a drink. We'd to go a 'somewhere else'. Really, it wasn't a decision. The Orchard was less than five minutes walk. Everywhere else was miles away. With heavy hearts, we slouched the shortest of journeys.

And, wouldn't you just know it, it was great. True, we needed a couple of visits, but I'd be lying if I said we didn't take to the place. We'd do our usual, turn up the back of half eight, and drink our first pint like it was fuel. Thereafter, we'd slow down, and start going on about something, something off the telly, or about books, the news or to do with our travelling. What with The Orchard being busier, it wasn't long before we got 'Are these seats taken?' Much as we wanted to, we couldn't very well turn round and say, 'Aye, they are. Away back to your rough books!' The young folk would sit themselves down. A lull in their conversation, that would be the time it takes to blink, and next thing they'd be introducing themselves. They'd ask about our printed t-shirts. Because of the t-shirts, the travelling, and some of the things we came away with – not without good reason did Noxie's old dear call us 'the two most left wing guys this side of Jesus' – me and Noxie developed a reputation. Young folk would pick an argument. That said, there was never any trouble. We knew our stuff. Just your bog standard Burchill, Benn and Chomsky, what Noxie called, 'grown-ups BBC', but for the kids, it might as well have been the sermon on the mount.

They'd go, 'You boys are for real, eh?'

We'd go, 'Aye?'

Because of the travelling, if you like, the ambassadorial thing, me and Noxie were fine with new folk. We knew the whens and hows of taking interest. True, it helped no end that folk seemed to like us. We'd get bought drinks. We protested, but folk still included us in their rounds. Nobody would hear of us returning the favour. We never pushed the matter. We'd the celebrity status of expeditionists.

Something else The Orchard had going for it was Flo, one of the barmaids. As you do, we started off fancying her, then, as you do, we started falling in love with her. Then we realised we didn't fancy her, and we weren't in love with her. Pure and simple, Flo, with that rare mix of calm, exotica and charm, was like somebody we'd've met abroad. She was about as native as ET. Flo had us send postcards of our travels. When we got back, she wanted to see photos. We let her keep the ones she wanted, and she pinned them up on the gantry, alongside the postcards and a couple of clippings.

We couldn't have gone back to The Belford. We couldn't have left Flo. And we couldn't have gone back to being unpopular. Ever since we'd moved, this thing kept happening: we'd sit there, and folk would come to us. Fair enough, sometimes it would be because they were wanting away from their company, and sometimes it would be because a certain somebody was already in our company. All the same, folk seemed to like us. If there was a party, we'd be invited. Me and Noxie, never renowned for putting it about, even partook of some hot teen action. We drew the line at girlfriends. The young folk respected this, but somehow took it to mean we'd be ideal agony uncles. Most had never been out of a relationship for more than 24 hours since they were twelve. They were keen to tell us their troubles. When enough was enough, we'd to do the time-out sign, and go, 'Too much information!', shaming them into shutting up. As for ourselves, our love lifes, and the lack thereof, Flo said we were too fussy, either that or we were gay. Regarding 'fussy', one time, Flo asked us what we thought about ten different lassies. We described each in turn as being 'alright'. Flo then asked us what we thought regarding a variety of crisp flavours. We were decidedly more animated. The gay thing was the usual. Two guys together. (Gay). Gigglers. (Gay). Tactless and bitchy. (Gay). Kilts. (Camp as knickers).

In saying this, and given what had gone before, we never had a problem with our new found popularity. We were the same as ever we were. Only thing was, we'd gone public. We became not so much regulars as fixtures of The Orchard. We met kids as sixth years, and seen them through to graduation. There was the odd concern. As Flo said, 'Wouldn't think it to look at youse, but you pair can be terrible for leading folk astray.'

Because of who we were, me and Noxie were deemed to be safe: no drugs, could hold our drink, and never got into bother. But, folk played games. There were those who hung around us to get away from their studying, or their partners, or because they didn't want to

p
110

t's a command performance fae yer man, a' the stories he couldnae tell

hazel irvine

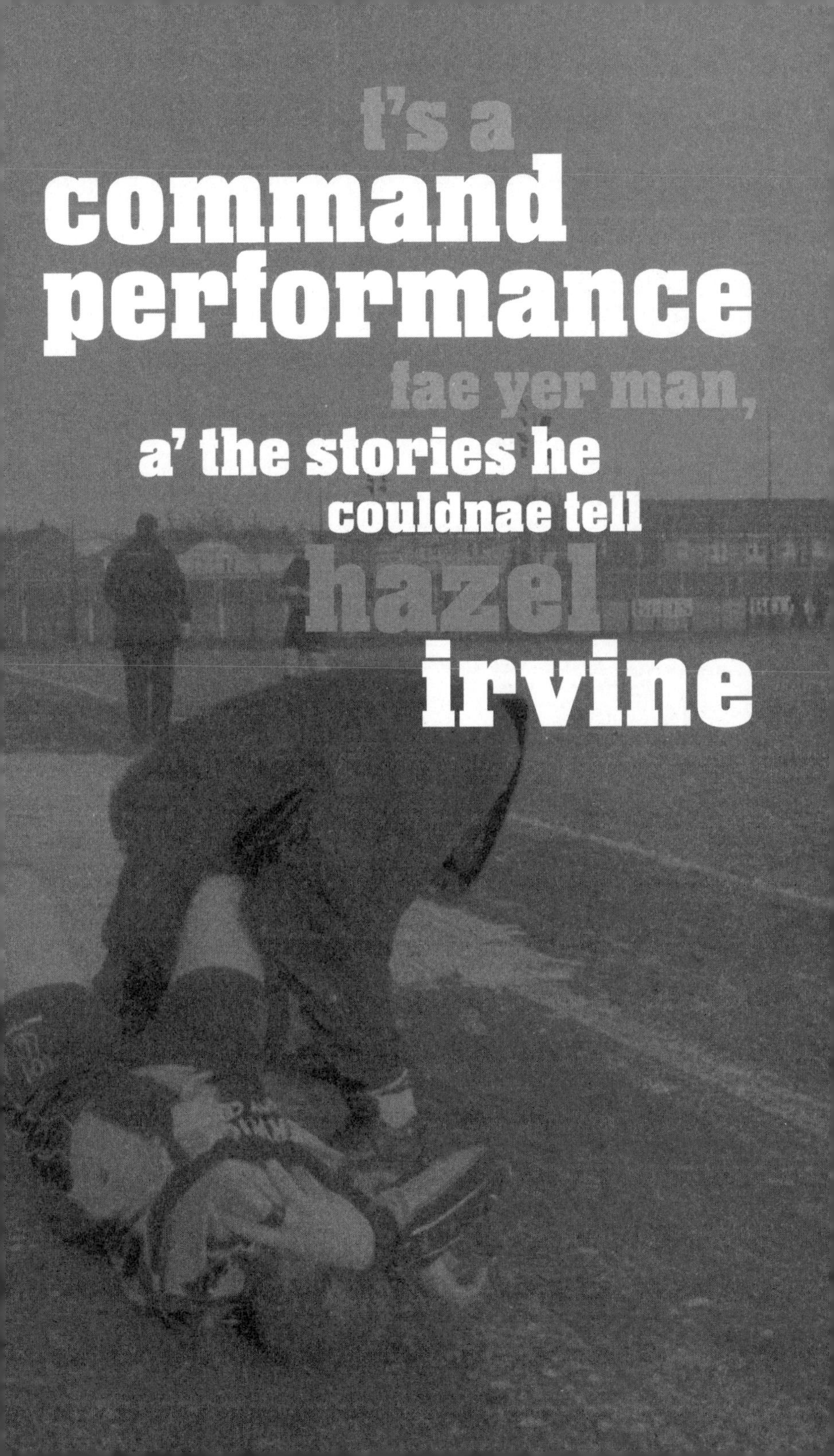

drink alone. For a good while there, it seemed like we knew everybody. You wanted anything, we knew where you'd get it. And no doubt we facilitated the odd estrangement. Not that every estrangement was a downfall.

Fred wouldn't have said so.

When it came to 'leading folk astray', Fred was the ultimate. He was the one we should've had least to worry about, too; yet he was the one who changed everything.

July, 2000, and a Saturday. We'd seen this guy the past couple of nights, up at the bar. He'd kept looking over.

I said to Noxie, 'See that?'

'Aye.'

'D'you ken him or something?'

'Nut.'

'He at your work?'

'Don't 'hink so. Yours?'

'Don't 'hink so.'

'Sure?'

'...'

'...'

'Nut. No' really.'

At long last, the guy came over. He'd his pint and, to implicate Flo, three packets of crisps.

Noxie ripped open one of the packets. He lay the open packet in front of the guy, and offered him first crisp. Noxie said, 'Sit yourself down, stranger. Feed your face and tell us all about yourself.' The guy took a handful of crisps. 'Funny,' he said, 'just by watching you pair, the look of you, I knew we were going to get on.'

'The look of you' bit was indeed 'funny'. The guy was like handsome and stuff, rich-looking. We were just your typical tattieheids: fat, balding, sticky out lugs, distinctly and extensively blotchy.

The guy introduced himself as being Fred. On account of what was on the gantry, and on account of him being English, Fred had been a bit wary of coming over. We saved him the lecture – 'We're not anti-English. We're not nationalists' – and told him just to get on with it.

Fred was working over at the Chemicals, an eighteen month contract. His company – note, *his* company – was building a plant at the end of Wholeflats. Fred was from Fareham, near Gosport, in Hampshire. His mother had been born in West Kilbride. The way he told it, Fred had always had a hankering for the old country. He was about our age but was was married with a couple of kids. His missus did 'a bit of modelling'. Fred showed us a photo.

Noxie said, 'Wee bit stunning, like.'

The plan was every fifth week Fred would take days off and head south. The rest of the time he'd be staying at The Orchard.

Me and Noxie looked at each other. We'd never met anybody who'd stayed at The Orchard. It wasn't something we'd ever thought about.

Given the time he was going to be around, and his obvious wealth, Noxie wondered whether Fred wouldn't be better renting somewhere, getting a lease on a wee castle or something.

Fred wasn't having it. 'No. This is tops, this is. Great big room. Wonderful meals. Great staff. Quite reasonable as well.'

Me and Noxie looked at each other again.

All our pubs were hotels.

Fred continued. Every day he got his sheets changed. Every day a bottle of water and a packet of wafer biscuits would be left on his pillow. He'd a trouser press, satellite telly and a heated bath, complete with power shower. A speaker in the en suite allowed him to keep tabs on radio or telly. The Orchard took care of his laundry. Fred said his room was the one directly above the main door. Me and Noxie had to think about that.

That night ended with a bit of a session. One of the students's sisters was having a 21st. With 'safety net rich mummy and daddy' away for the weekend, we were all invited back to the family house. To begin with, Fred was reluctant. We assured him, at such gatherings, tradition favoured the appearance of a gormless out-of-towner that nobody had ever heard of. Fred took this as his invite. From the bar, he got a bottle of champagne, and offered to pay our share of the carry out. Me and Noxie said, 'On you go.' Fred was obviously used to folk haggling over such matters, and thought we were being funny. We weren't. As with our occasional takeaways, the rationale was you paid in relation to what you could afford.

Fred laughed. 'You guys are for real, eh?'

We said, 'Aye?'

As far as these affairs went, the party was fine. Fred gave a sterling performance of 'man who doesn't get out much'. He got drunk really quickly, then moved on to tea and toast, then got drunk again. Everybody loved him. He kept on about me and Noxie: our travels, the gantry, and our printed t-shirts. That night, I was sporting a picture of Mayakovski, while Noxie's said, 'If you take out all the shoulds, what's left that's worth anything?'

Come five in the morning, it was time to go. Those who hadn't fallen asleep, were tidying up, busying themselves till The Grange opened at six. Fred seemed keen on The Grange, and in particular its chin high sinks ('What? To stop folk pissing in them?'), but, by then, the poor fellow had barely a clue left about anything.

All night, Fred had went on about this eighteen months of his, and how me and Noxie were going to be his pals. With respect to our travelling, he kept saying, 'I'm coming with youse! I'm coming with youse!' We humoured him. Folk were always 'coming with youse'. They never did.

We walked Fred back to The Orchard. He pointed out his room, like he'd said, the one above the main entrance, which, when you saw it, clearly was the main entrance. The sign above the door – 'The Orchard Hotel' – being a bit of a giveaway. For what seemed like the first time, we noticed how our bit, and its side entrance and public bar, was merely a jumped-up shoe-box that had attached itself, probably with an allen key, to the original four-storey building.

Now I knew how the kids who spent their schooldays being taught in huts felt.

Fred meanwhile, wanted a group hug. Noxie, trying to be emphatic, said, 'Let's no' go there, eh?'

But Fred wasn't big on impulse control. He wrapped his arms round us and hauled us in, 'I'm coming with youse! I'm coming with youse!'

There had to be better ways of spending five minutes.

Eventually, we saw Fred off. We watched as he let himself in The

Orchard's main entrance.

I said, 'He's got a key!'

I said it the same way folk in films sometimes turn round and say, 'He's got a gun!'

The upshot was, Fred did indeed become our pal. He was around for our nights out, and remained insistent that he was coming on our travels: so much so, and here's money for you, he even went out and got tickets. Like I say, everybody loved him. Fred could do that thing that always eluded me and Noxie, he could instigate. By way of example: say we were out and a song came on. Within the first few bars, Fred would go, 'Oh, I love that!' Invariably, somebody else would go, 'I love that, too. It's my favourite.' Fred and whoever would bond. In the same circumstance, when it came to expressing an opinion, me and Noxie could've only ever've went, 'I fucking hate that!' Consequently, me and Noxie didn't really do bonding. Another thing Fred could do, he could flirt. He said it was because he was married. He said, being married let you flirt and get away with it. Me and Noxie nodded – yeah, like we understand.

Yet, for all he'd his own company, the house the size of Southfork, the kids, the 'wee bit stunning' wife, and the looks and social skills to die for, Fred had never had pals. He'd went from school to uni. The day after graduation, Fred had got married. He had slaved his guts out to make some rich cunt richer, only, in this instance, the rich cunt was himself. The way Fred told it, he'd hardly did anything. He'd never been to a football match. He'd never travelled anywhere that hadn't involved work or family. That was what 'I'm coming with youse!' was all about: Fred was set to join us on our travels. This time round, the qualifying campaign for the 2002 World Cup. All being well, the three of us would be spending early summer, 2002, in Japan and Korea. Fred thought this was dream come true stuff. And so did we.

Ever since we were bairns, all me and Noxie ever wanted to do was follow the national team. When we realised all we needed was money, and a wee bit gumption, we went for it. Domestically, football-wise, we were never that bothered. A pound-fifty day-saver could get us to and from any one of three senior grounds, albeit lower league ones, and a reasonably successful junior side. Over the years we'd had a go at supporting each of them, but, with the passing of time, the less we went. Fred was keen though, so we chummed him along.

Domestic football was a struggle for me and Noxie. We were unashamed snobs. We'd nothing in common with half these people. Some of them were just plain offensive. For them, opposition supporters were 'scum', opposition forwards were 'cheats', opposition defenders were 'animals', while match officials were 'bent bastards'. People forever claimed decisions that were anything but.

Fred pointed out how it was the same few folk dishing out the barbs. He'd been more interested in, and fascinated by, what was happening on the pitch; as, it has to be said, was the bulk of the crowd. Me and Noxie apologised. 'Is it not,' he said, 'just a case of empty barrels? Somewhere a scheme is missing its idiot?'

We apologised again. Thing was, the local team, our team, was getting beat. If they'd been winning, the terracing comment would've been funny. This was something that always bugged me and Noxie.

The following weekend, Fred took off to see his family. He needed the break. Most days, Fred had barely a moment to himself. Through the week, after work, he'd be on the phone to me and Noxie, wanting to go to the pictures, or find a gym, or just rent a car and head off somewhere. I told him to veg: 'Fred, man, you've satellite telly! Chill!' Noxie though – Mr Wuss when it came to the old KB – went out a few times, to the gym, the pictures, for drives, whatever.

When he returned from down south, Noxie had Fred round for tea. With the qualifying campaign getting ever closer, there were a few things Fred could probably've been done with being told about.

One of which would've been this video Noxie's old dear's got. Stuff she'd taped off the telly. All the highlights from our campaigns. Me and Noxie in Mexico, getting interviewed by the BBC. Me and Noxie in Spain, sat on the terraces, heads in laps. Me and Noxie behind the bloke that got kissed by the Swedish police lassie. Me and Noxie sambaing with some serious Brazilians. Loads of this kind of stuff.

There was also a scrapbook. The scrapbook was the size of a mattress.

Whenever we went abroad, me and Noxie had to find a barbers and get our heads shaved. Our old dears made us do it. They reasoned, if we were going to do all this then somebody was as well to benefit. Before we left we'd to go round with the sponsor sheets. What, with me at the hospital, Noxie out and about with the council, and our old dears being active, we done alright. To date, we'd raised £50,000+ for the local hospice. We'd had our heads shaved in thirty seven different countries. The local paper always carried a piece. Most of the nationals had featured us as well.

That night, I arrived just as Fred was reading about one of our orphanages. For a while, it seemed we couldn't look out Jimmy wigs without having to build a flaming orphanage.

Fred said, 'You boys are for real, eh?'

Me and Noxie said, 'Aye?'

We gave it the usual, moaning about how the papers misquoted us, when what we'd actually said was how there should be no such thing as charity, and how everybody's needs should be met by taxation and central government. We'd been suckered with the orphanages as well. Classic western foreign policy, turn up, be the white man, start something off, and leave a mess behind.

Noxie's old dear put on the other video she'd got, the one she called, 'The two most left wing guys this side of Jesus.'

Me and Noxie lobbing bricks at Wopping. Me and Noxie getting lifted at Faslane. Me and Noxie getting lifted at Timex. Me and Noxie getting lifted at Bilston Glen. Me and Noxie getting lifted at Glasgow's George Square (though none of us could remember exactly what it was we were protesting about). There was tons of that stuff as well, dating back to schooldays.

This was plain embarrassing. I got up, stretched myself, and started rattling my keys. Drink beckoned.

Noxie's old dear said, 'That'll be youse then, eh? Well, it was nice to've met you, Fred, son. And I hope you get as much out of the travelling as this pair.'

'Can hardly wait. Can't believe the first game's a fortnight.'

'And you'll have you got yourself kitted out?'

Fred looked blank.

He looked at us.

We looked blank as well.

'Richardson's,' said Noxie's old dear. 'The Royal Mile. If they can't get you sorted, nobody can. Mind and mind your cheque book.'

Fred now looked alarmingly blank.

I helped out. 'We're going through Saturday. It was supposed to be a surprise.'

Fred look scared.

Me and Noxie went, 'Surprise!!!!!'

Fred looked really scared.

Down the pub, once he realised what was happening, Fred traded 'scared' for a serious attack of the death rows. It was alright being pals and everything, doing the travelling, but this was maybe a bit much. He said, 'Could I maybe not just wear my jeans?'

With everybody wanting to know why me and Noxie were pissing ourselves, the secret was out. The lassies told Fred how he'd look fantastic. One boy told him about the 'change'.

Fred said, 'Change?'.

'Mystical,' the boy said. 'Spiritual. Things happen.'

We said not to worry. It was just a wind-up. Nothing more dramatic was going to happen than not having any pockets, that was all.

There wasn't much in the way of browsing matter at Richardsons – postcards, trinkets, rizla-thin tourist publications. The rest of the place, the size of a mini-market, was devoted to what was called 'attire'.

'Seen the price of this?' Fred was fingering a Prince Charlie coatee. Since we'd arrived, he'd been moaning about prices, like he was poor or something.

'Rich boy pish,' said Noxie.

Fred grunted.

An assistant approached us. His name badge said 'Mr Givens'. Assured and disarmingly pleasant, Mr Givens had the appearance and retired military bearing of Gordon Jackson out of The

Professionals. Mr Givens addressed Fred. 'Good morning, sir. Now what can we do for you?'

Earlier, me and Noxie had told Fred we weren't going to help him. All he was doing was shopping. Surely, he'd been shopping before. Surely, he'd had to buy the 'wee bit stunning' wife lingerie or whatever. Surely, that had to be ten times more embarrassing than this. Fred said he'd never had to buy his wife lingerie. What with the modeling, she got all her gear for free. She'd 'tons of really expensive lingerie'. That was the moment – 'tons of really expensive lingerie' – when me and Noxie thought nah, you're doing this on your own, pal.

Mr Givens smiled. Mr Givens waited. Mr Givens could sniff a credit card limit at ten paces. The limit on Fred's card said, 'sky'.

Finally, Fred spoke. 'I'm here to buy a kilt.'

'Good gosh,' said Mr Givens. 'That wasn't so hard, was it? Now, I'm wondering, have you any particular tartan in mind?'

'No.'

Mr Givens continued. 'Very well, let me explain. While there are no strict rules governing the wearing of Highland Dress, there are, as you'll find with any form of attire, certain conventions which the paying customer may feel obliged to adhere to. For example, the wearing of a specific tartan may indicate a longstanding familial or geographical connection. Many family names, alas without tartans themselves, have strong associations with particular Highland Clans, and customers often choose to wear the tartan of said clan.' Mr Givens paused. 'I'm wondering, a family name perhaps?'

Fred said, 'De Vries. Frederick Algernon de Vries.'

Mr Givens smiled. 'No, laddie, that would be the continental lowlands.'

This could've went on and on.

'Your mother,' I said to Fred. 'Your mother's maiden name.'

'Grier,' said Fred. 'Avril Stevenson Grier.'

'Grier?' Mr Givens was excited... 'My goodness. You know that's a McGregor, don't you?'

'Aye?' Fred was excited, too.

'I'm sure of it. Very strong connections, very strong. Excuse me a second.'

The tension! It was like waiting for somebody to take their shot at snooker.

'Yes,' said Mr Givens. He was over by the till, flicking through a glossy loose leaf tome, like one of the in-store Argos catalogues. 'McGregor it is. Congratulations.'

Fred whispered, 'McGregor. I'm a McGregor.' Then he said it again. Only this time, loud.

'McGregor!! I'm a McGregor!!'

Over by the door, a couple of browsing Scandinavians decided they had to be going.

Already, Fred was on the 'change'. His feet had gone to ten to two. His hands were on his hips.

Fred said, 'Amazing, eh? So, what is it? Wee bit rumpy pumpy in the haystacks? Some doomed love affair between Rob Roy and some servant wench? Next thing you know bob's your uncle?'

(Noxie whispered, 'What, Bob Roy McGregor's your uncle?')

Mr Givens was flicking through his Argos, as though he was deciding whether his commission should go on a new bathroom suite or a nest of tables for the lobby. Mr Givens continued, 'While many connections between clans and what are known as septs, associated names, can, at times, be quite tenuous, and, if you'll beg the pardon – and this is purely a personal view – on occasions, be frankly damn silly, in this instance, the connection does appear to be very strong. I'd say almost to the point of incontrovertible. It dates back centuries, you know. Quite fascinating.'

'Quite fascinating,' agreed Fred.

'Now,' Mr Givens closed his book. 'You'll be pleased to hear, we have a choice of two McGregors. We have the formal evening McGregor, and,' and, at this point, Mr Givens paused a truly great pause, 'and,' he said, 'we have of course' – another pause – 'the famous fishing, hunting and fighting McGregor!'

At this point, Fred turned into Homer McSimpson. Three wee thought bubbles popped out the back of his head. One going, 'Fishing!' One going 'Hunting!' And one going 'Fighting!'

Fred cleared his throat. 'I'm wondering,' he said, 'would it be at all possible to see an example of the famous fishing, hunting and fighting?'

Mr Givens – who Noxie later told me later he'd thought of throughout as being Mr Crivens – said, 'Bear with me.'

Mr Givens headed off.

Fred turned to us. 'You boys got a fishing, hunting and fighting?'

It was a good three hours before we finally got away. In between times, we managed a Mexican and a visit to The People's Story. When we returned, Fred had his fishing, hunting and fighting ready for him, along with a Jacobite shirt, and appropriate socks and shoes. We reminded him he wasn't going to a wedding.

When he first tried on the 'attire' I said, 'Fred, you don't normally watch your knees when you walk, do you?'

Mr Givens was a tad blunter. 'Straighten yourself, laddie. You're not a lummox, you're a McGregor.'

Once he'd parted with half his fortune, Fred had one last anxious query. 'Tell me, you being the man and all of that, what's supposed to go underneath?'

Mr Givens smiled. 'As previously stated, as with any form of attire, Highland Dress is entirely a matter of taste.' Mr Givens cast a disapproving eye at mine's and Noxie's t-shirts. I'd my Church of John Coltrane. Noxie's was a picture of Elvis Presley's last prescription. 'Regardless of what lies beneath the kilt, one should never admit to wearing anything. At all times, maintain the mystique. If I could possibly be so bold as to suggest a couple of the more acceptable responses. For example, should a lady ask what is worn beneath your kilt, you are perfectly within your rights to say, 'Nothing worn, ma'am. Everything in perfect working order.' While, on the other hand, if a gentleman makes the same enquiry, the response should be, Sir, nothing so much as your fair maiden's lipstick and a dash of her bonny saliva.'

Mr Givens had a wee chuckle to himself. You could tell he liked a chuckle.

That night, back at The Orchard, we got hammered, mightily. Fred had on his 'attire'. He looked stunning. The jokes were working, too. All you'd hear would be 'a dash of her bonny saliva', then a burst of laughter that could break down walls. One of the students had a new one. In response to a female inquisitor you were 'perfectly within your rights' to say, 'I'm a man of few words, lass. Gie's your hand.'

Time was when me and Noxie would've found all this to be the epitomy of naff. To be part of it though, like when we were away, could actually be quite wonderful. This night, Fred's night, was one such.

And there was only one way to finish.

The climax had me, Noxie and Fred up on top of one of the tables, belting out, to the tune of The Monkees 'I'm a Believer', our new anthem, the frankly wonderful, 'I'm a McGregor'.

The next time we did our three tenors we were in Riga. We'd a new song ('We hate Coca Cola/We hate Fanta too/We're the Tartan Army/We drink Irn Bru') and new t-shirts. Mine's was, 'Beware! Premature Jock Elation!' Noxie's was Richard Brautigan's poem about how come all Japanese women are beautiful. Even Fred had a printed t-shirt he'd got off of the internet: a picture of history's most famous fisted goal, inscribed with the legend 'The Hand of God Squad'.

If there's a pub on Mars, it'll be an Irish one. In Riga, we headed for The Third Policeman. Having spent so much time with us, Fred, like that book's bicycle, was slowly turning into us. First thing he said when we hit the town centre: 'Latvian women are stunning, eh.'

'Second only to Lithuanians,' pointed out Noxie.

To be fair, wherever we went, indigenous males weren't shy about praising our women. Me and Noxie could do a good downer when it came to our homeland. Our mountains were hills. Our cities were scaffolding. Our claim to fame was a tea towel list of inventors who got credit for inventing things that almost certainly would've got invented anyway - well, with the possible exception of golf.

When we were away, all folk ever asked us was, 'What's the best whisky?'

Like, what's the best blade of grass.

In the modern age, we'd the world's best national dress, and the world's best behaved national football fans. Both of which came about by default. We never used to wear the kilt, and we never used to be well-behaved. Noxie gave Fred a run-down of the do's and don'ts of self-policing.

'Any of ours is a pain in the arse, we get a team together and sort them out. Any of ours is in trouble, we help them out. Be wary of 'characters', especially those that've made it here under their own steam: chances are, authorities somewhere are presently looking for them. Smile and say hello to everybody. Be seen to point at and photograph any building bigger than a bus shelter. Give money to beggars, talk to them, and, at all times, look like you're having the time of your life. Think of it as a pageant, and that everybody's pleased to see you.'

'Jesus,' said Fred.

'And,' added Noxie 'anybody's building a hospital or an orphanage, we've to be seen to be lending a hand. Even if it means missing our connections. Actually, especially if it means missing our connections.'

'So we stay in the pub then?' said Fred.

'Too fucking right,' said Noxie. 'Couple of hours sightseeing, gets the heads shaved, then down the pub.'

We got a late, undeserved winner in Riga. Fred had never experienced the like. To've been part of such a crowd, who, through every last moment of the ninety odd minutes, had endured exactly the same frustrations, disappointments and grievances, right up until that ultimate release of joy and euphoria, had been nothing less than physical poetry. Fred was drained.

'Aye,' said Noxie. 'Socialism used to be like that.'

Two late goals scraped us a win in San Marino. We'd bother beforehand when some knobend took exception to Fred's accent. Within seconds, a team of boys from Kelty was on the scene, and the knobend was removed.

In Croatia, we met boys from Ardrossan who were working on a water purification scheme. We gave them a hand, got photos taken, and Fred made a couple of calls. As for the game, the draw was well-earned, against one of the classier sides we could've come up against. Fred said he'd never concentrated so much in his life. After –

and I'm not allowed to say where – we met Croatian playmaker Robert Prosineski, and got photos taken with him. He looked about as fit as me, too.

Back home, Fred was full of stories. He'd come away with stuff, and me and Noxie would be thinking, that's right, and we were there!!!

Fred's involvement increased our charity revenue tenfold. We got more publicity than we'd had in years. Down south, Fred's local rag ran a feature, as did one of the lad's mags. The fact Fred's company got mentioned everywhere kind of went against the grain, but, swings and roundabouts, if it hadn't been for that we wouldn't have got so much money.

To keep us going till the next cluster of games, we'd work, our three nights out, and our books, tellys and phones. So far, we'd good results. We needed the dream come true one.

One night, just before Christmas, post pub and pakora, at the junction of Inchyra and Wholeflats, me and Noxie were talking about this, going to Belgium and beating them.

There followed one of our sleepy-eyed, yawn stifling silences.

As it started to rain, the sun came out. Noxie picked up the thread.

'Look,' he said, 'a couple of things've been happening. I've been meaning to tell you.'

Noxie paused a Givens-like pause.

'I've been seeing somebody. Lassie from my work. Three months now. We're thinking of getting a place. I should've mentioned it, sorry, but, ken what it's like, you don't want to put the hex on things. I feel really crap about this.'

I couldn't think of what to say.

'Listen,' he said. 'I'll no' be down the pub so much.'

I said, 'It's okay. I've always got Fred.'

Noxie went all Givens again.

'Fred and Flo are an item. Have been a while now. They're going to go public quite soon.'

It was my turn for the dramatic pause.

'But is he no' supposed to be married or something?'

'Yeah, he's married, but they're not together. They weren't together when we first met him. He wasn't sure what was happening. She's with somebody else now. Some doctor. Apparently, they're okay about it. Just too much, too young. You know.' Noxie stopped. 'Ken this is difficult. You've been treated like shite. Sorry.'

Noxie had changed. I could see it now. There was me thinking it was him and Fred down the gym. He'd lost weight, he'd decent clothes. He wasn't phoning so much. He was hardly in when I phoned. His old dear said he was with Fred.

Noxie said. 'Alright?'

'Yeah. Eh, aye.'

I was shaking.

All our days, me and Noxie only ever talked about things, never about ourselves, not really. Couple of times, early on, and that would've been primary school, we'd went in the huff with each other, but we'd never once fell out. That would've been us over and done with. There was just way too much baggage. As much as this was doing my head in, it was cutting him to pieces.

Noxie said, 'I'm no' sure about what's happening with the travelling. You know, money.'

The only thing stopping me from greeting was knowing he would start as well. I couldn't do that. I couldn't say, 'But, hold on, you always said...' Things had changed. The past was a foreign country. More than anybody, we knew that.

'Look,' said Noxie, 'there's introductions to be made. I need to get that sorted. I'll phone you, right?'

I went over and hugged him. The guy was rigid. 'Pleased for you, mate,' I said. 'Mean that. Just feeling a bit shite for myself, that's all.'

Noxie remained rigid. I could feel the floodgates coming, and headed off.

Things being things, they just got worse and worse.

At work, I got promoted, to what they called team leader. But with us now being a contracted company, as opposed to a department, even though it was the same folk doing the same jobs, we could no longer do things the way we'd always done them. To save money, the workload got bigger and the staff got reduced. I'd to explain policies I didn't understand. I'd to implement procedures I didn't agree with.

Even if Matt was a

Catholic

that was only

the reason the door had

never

p

122

and Willie a

Protestant,

half

been breached.

Noxie got me round. I met Fiona. She was lovely and everything, and, despite the awkwardness, we got on fine. We went out a few times, and she got mates of hers to come along. I felt like somebody else was putting my clothes on for me.

Mind you, that was shootie-in compared with going back to The Orchard. All these new photos were up on the gantry.

Flo said, 'Okay?'

'Yeah. Just found out I'm adopted. My real dad's Kevin Keegan. They won't tell me who my mum is. They're worried it might upset me.'

Flo laughed. We could always make each other laugh. She leant over and gave me a kiss.

I could've done without that. Fred and me had a chat. I could probably've done without that as well. Fred filled me in about his marriage. Him and Flo had been together since the night of the 'fishing, hunting and fighting'. The night of the 'change'. Fred told me he loved her. She looked like she loved him. I felt crap. I'd lost my friends.

The next two games were home ones, Belgium and San Marino. We were two up against Belgium within half an hour. We needed a third, but Belgium pulled one back on the hour. The longer it went on, the more likely it was they would score. Belgium equalised in the 90th minute. Noxie and Fred took it bad. Noxie was raging. He wasn't alone. Sometimes being part of a like-minded crowd isn't necessarily pleasant. We got a victory over San Marino, but that was to be expected.

I started going to The Grange. With no Noxie, and nothing to say, I ended up just drinking. Me and Noxie always said, regardless of where you were, bars were the only places where you never had to repeat yourself when you asked for something.

I made enquiries about getting a mail order bride, save somebody from having to eke out a living in some Gap or Nike sweatshop. I couldn't go through with it. I thought about doing away with myself. I couldn't go through with that either.

Noxie's old dear phoned. She hadn't seen me in ages. She said I needed to do something. She didn't like the idea I was like this. She said my family was worried about me.

I couldn't think what to do. I didn't want to be a blooterheid. During the summer, Noxie and Fiona got a house, and announced they were getting married, Fred and Flo got a house, and announced Fred was getting divorced. I gave up the drink and started doing loads of overtime. All I did was work, sleep and work. The final three games came round. We drew at home to Croatia, which was fine, at least we hadn't got beat. The big one was next, over in Belgium. Thinking it might bring some Riga-type luck, Fred got us all 'The Hand of God Squad' t-shirts. The cameras picked us out. We got beat 2–0. The better side won. As we were leaving, an old guy said, 'Had us fooled again, eh?' He started singing, 'We'll support you ever more.' We'd a final game, at home to Latvia, but only a fluke result elsewhere would've seen us through. It never happened.

We weren't going to Japan and Korea.

Of the eight games, we'd lost only one.

In days gone by, that would've been us back to our Thursday through Saturdays, or our Fridays through Sundays, and our books, tellys and phones, waiting for the draw for the European Championships.

Flo phoned, saying she was keeping tabs on errant customers. She slagged me for still staying with my folks. She slagged me for not having a girlfriend. She slagged me for stopping drinking.

I told her about me and Noxie first meeting her, about how we fancied her, and how we grew to fall in love with her, but then how, with the passing of time, we thought she was like somebody we'd have met abroad. I don't suppose I made a good job of explaining it.

Flo said, 'I think I prefer the idea of you having fancied me. You're never going to get the hang of this, are you?'

It wasn't a great call.

Really, I had to do something, get the hang of something, something I wanted to do. I started raking through my stuff: tickets, programmes, scraps of paper. I got through the phone book and checked the hundred or so bar-code sized numbers. Eventually, I found the one I wanted. This was a guy from last campaign but one, an ex-pat. He was giving it a few years then selling up. He wasn't coming back – 'Fuck that' he'd said – he was just retiring. He was off to travel the world. Properly, this time.

I dialled the number. I kept telling myself I wasn't running away. That would've been like saying Noxie and Fred had ran away. All it was was they'd done things they wanted to do. Same as I wanted to do this, what me and Noxie had always talked about. Our Shangri-la, our earthly paradise. A dream come true.

The call went fine. The guy remembered me. He'd other parties interested, but nobody was battering down the door.

It took months to get sorted. I kept up the overtime. Me being boss, nobody else got a look in. I was tired but I felt good. When the time came, I handed in my notice. I told my folks, but asked them not to tell anybody. I couldn't tell Noxie and Fred. I'd started off feeling obliged doing this, but now I was excited.

I got my money. Ever since we'd left school me and Noxie had put money away, starting with that hundred a month. Folk laughed at us. But it was all there, and then some. I was no Fred, but I wasn't poor.

A year on from the Belgium game, I made my move. By now, I'd come to terms with a lot of stuff. Maybe, more importantly, I'd come to terms with myself. I'd changed.

And I think that's something that'll continue.

I didn't do anything about getting in touch. I left it for a couple of months. Just too busy. I put together two postcards from photos of the place.

Me and Noxie had a dream of running a bar, and decorating it with the stuff from our travels. We'd talk about where we wanted it to be. But we always came back to one favourite.

In the two photos-come-postcards, the sign says 'Fred + Noxie's'. Really, I couldn't think what else to call it. A crap working title became an official name.

One of the postcards was for Noxie and Fiona, the other for Fred and Flo. I put the same message on each.

As yet, they've not replied. To be honest, I prefer to imagine their news. I'm a Scotland football supporter. I'm a sentimentalist. They'll be busy. Being here, doing this, I'm loving it. I understand what my predecessor meant. I'm not going back.

It is a dream come true. But there's another one, another dream.

One day, doesn't matter when, some strange looking visitors'll turn up on the doorstep. It'll take a second to figure out who we all are.

But once we do, we'll greet our eyes out.

Alright?

...and welcome to next street but one to the KGB museum!

I'm happy! I'm busy!

The talent's stunning, but – pity – I'm getting used to it.

I am not single!!!

Should see this place. Photos everywhere. Looks great. Business is booming.

Take care. Hope you're well. All the best. Love you loads...

'The Second Most Left Wing Guy This Side Of Jesus'
Vilnius 2002

P.S. Nearly forgot. This place is a hotel. See you when I see you.

The Cherrypicker

Jim Carruthers

Learn to read.
A wrong guess will
cost ye cups.

I never really worked out whether I believed him. Once he started reminiscing, I listened with wonder to his stories of another place where everybody had a bunnet, women barely existed and pies were built to last. Scotland in the twenties.

'Did ye ken ah wuz a cherrypicker?' he growled. I watched the sunlight steer through the wee window and catch the blue smoke idling from his fag.

He raised himself noisily out of his armchair and got the photos down from the mantelpiece. He took time to launch a clocher at the fire. It fizzled like a melting marble.

'See, there's Shanks, I telt ye he stopped by last week. Still in good form.'

He handled the photos with such care, more than he would ever direct at me or any of his other grandchildren.

Every time he showed me the photos, I couldn't recognise him, never mind anyone else.

Life was fairly drab in the early sixties, but at the time of the photos it must have been awful. The team looked so hard, each player eyeing up the camera for a square go. Arms folded with a regimented and style free hairdo. The strips were hooped. Were it not for the shorts in the front row, you would have thought they were away to break rocks in a penal colony.

'Noo away and practise in the byre. Keep daein that and ye micht be as guid as me. Failin' that ye micht turn oot as usefae as yur Uncle Wullie. Feed the hens while yur oot there an fetch some coal back wae ye, div ye hear?'

I loved playing with that wee ball in the byre. It came off the stone walls at funny angles, always keeping you on your toes. Like he said, it was good practice. Nimble like a ballet dancer. Learn to read. A wrong guess will cost ye cups. Niver heed that Brazilian stuff.

'Div ye hear?' His coaching came, like most of his demands with this added. It was all like that then; my folks, my teachers, the school team manager. On your back and barking.

In the byre it never rained or felt cold. The practice always ended up at Wembley, where I scored the settling penalty, just inside the tattie-barrel post. Giving it enough height so it didn't catch the edge of the byre drain. Keeping it down so it didn't hit the wood that came half down the wall. It made it easy for the goalkeeper to save if it was that high.

When I went in he was asleep. I put the bucket down and added a few nuggets to the fire. I stubbed out the smoulder that came from his ashtray. For no reason I said cheerio as I left.

He died in October 67, not long after the summer of joy. The death certificate said cirrhosis and pneumonia. Being sixteen and still ignorant, I was sure it was more to do with fags and mouldy food. I was all excited at the prospect of the funeral. Nobody famous came. However one old man had come over from Ayrshire.

He eyed me, 'So you're his grandson then?' He shook my hand with strength and vigour. Mine was limp with hope.

'Are you alright, you're clammy?'

'Fine, I think. Eh – are you from Glenbuck?' I spluttered back.

'God no mun, I'm from Cumnock.'

'Were you a cherrypicker then?'

'Naw lad, I only played with him in the army. And if you are asking, he was good, he was good. Good enough indeed.' He winked at me and emptied his glass with a decided flourish. Excusing himself he went off to find more whisky. I never got to speak to him again.

After it was over, I got hold of the old iron key to the cottage and raked round the place like a detective. In truth it felt more like a burglary. There had to be some confirming evidence, a medal or letter. I went into the room where he slept before the bed was moved through. There were tins and boxes but nothing, not even a postcard from Liverpool. I reasoned that there could be something but it was just lost to the mildew and stains that were all over the room.

Years later, I stumbled across Glenbuck. The whole area was derelict. Abandoned workings. Uninhabitable houses. Although the sun shone over the rank moorland that surrounded the desolation, it was cold. A penal colony would have had more charm.

Cherry trees? Impossible. Something that swept the air with fragrance and produced single shots of summer juice.

Never.

Nae Cunt Said Anyhin

Andrew C Ferguson

wan minute it wis fleein,
the next it seems tae take aff,
like a UFO

The first time I saw Tam dae magic on the ba was wi Ferrytoon Juniors. He just did enough, just enough so's we won the game, and that was it. And nae cunt said anyhin.

I'd been promotit fae the second team because they had a late call off, eh. Most ae these guys were eighteen, nineteen; a couple ae mair experienced cunts, but maist ae them just a couple ae years aulder than me. They pit me up front.

'Just run ontae Tam's ba's,' the captain said.

I started tae laugh.

'Run ontae his ba's?' Nae cunt else was laughin, though. Tam wis away the other end ae the dressin room, pitten Wintergreen on and talkin tae his mate.

'Aye, says the captain. You're supposed tae be quick, so be quick, son. And dinnae take any shite fae that big cunt that plays sweeper for them. He's a' mooth.'

Even then, Tam Johnston was one o thae midfield general types, eh. Swaggerin aboot wi the ba as if he owned the centre ae the park. Which in Tam's case he did.

First twenty minutes ae the game, we were just sittin in. We were second top, Buckhaven Royal Albert were relegation favourites. I got a couple ae square ba's fae Tam, and a load ae shite fae their sweeper. Captain was right aboot him. Big cunt, tae.

After half an hour, Tam comes up tae me while we're getting the ba off the road.

'Ye need tae be further up the park, son. Ah cannae pit ye through if ye're jined at the hip tae me.'

Ah look ower at the captain. He just gies me a look.

Ah didnae say anyhin, but I did get further up the park, eh, and Tam starts sprayin the ba aboot. He's playin these wee chipped passes intae space, ontae the edge ae the box, findin the gaps. The first couple I dinnae get ontae quick enough, and I'm closed doon by the big cunt ae a sweeper. Tam looks at the captain as if tae say, Ah cannae dae nuhin wi this cunt.

Third time I'm quicker, and the sweeper has tae clatter me fae behind. Tam helps me up. Free kick's wastit though. Tam melts it straight intae the wa. Gets the sweeper right in the nads though, funnily enough.

Next time, just afore half time, I'm waitin for it. Tam drifts up tae the centre circle, he's lost his marker and the defence is giein him tae much space. The sweeper's on me but ye can hear his brain grindin. Eventually, he goes for Tam and I make ma run. Tam dinks this wee ba right ower the sweeper's heid, it comes ower ma shoudir and Ah lash it past the oncoming keeper. Top corner. A stoater.

1–0 tae us, and pats oan the heid for yours truly. Except fae Tam, who just gies me a nod as if tae say, even you couldnae ae missed that. Big beetle-browed basturt, as the sweeper ca'd him when he was rollin aboot on the grund.

So I was kept oan for the second half and we started playin some fitba. Like I say, maist ae the boys in the first team were Tam's age, grew up together and that. Barry wee team at the time – should ae done mair, even after Tam moved oan up.

Ten minutes intae the second half, the sweeper pits me up in the air again, and the ref sends the big cunt aff. So, just the usual, we take our fit aff the gas, and the ten men start playin out o their skins. Five minutes later, they've got a jammy goal and it's backs tae the wa. Then we get a breakaway goal; long ba fae Tam which I chase doon, nutmeg their wingback and square tae oor winger for a tap-in. 2–1.

Still backs tae the wa. Tam disnae like defendin, eh.

'Get up the park, get up the fuckin park,' he's sayin tae me under his breath at the corners. Then he gets a brekk up the park himsel and wins a free kick, about twenty yards oot. And that's when he uses the magic, eh.

Tam wis a barry footballer already, like. Loads ae skill, strength on the ba, guid vision. There'd been scouts fae Premier clubs watchin him afore that game. But that free kick must ae done it. He signed the week eftir.

Tam takes the free kick, eh. Bent it roond the wa. Fair enough. There were other Ferrytoon boys could dae that wi a free kick. Outside ae the boot, specially if you've got a pair ae thae Predators oan.

But their keeper thinks he has it covered. He's actually placed the wa properly, and noo he dives right tae where the ba's going. Then the ba starts tae blur.

Noo, I ken in the paper reporters gan oan aboot the ba blurrin intae the net. But this wan really did; wan minute it wis fleein, the next it seems tae take aff, like a UFO or somehin, bent the ither way, under the keeper's body. Endae story. Buckhyne's heids gan doon eftir that, and we stroll it.

Weirdest thing aboot that free kick though, was that nae cunt said anyhin aboot it. It wis just like, that never happened, did it? Pats oan the back a' roond fur Tam, but nae cunt says, Tam, hoo did ye get the ba tae brekk every law ae physics like? Naebody.

Well, every cunt in Scotland kens whit happened tae Tam Johnston no long eftir. Signs for Rangers, eh. Wan and only Scottish player in the side, some games. Swaggers aboot the middle ae the park as if he owns it. Wins the treble wi them, next year the double. Gets ca'd up fur Scotland except they're so shite even Tam cannae make a difference. Couldnae score on Loveboat.

And we a' ken the rest ae the story tae. George Best oan a budget, oor Tam. Major pishheid, like. Turns up fur trainin pished, and gets the sack fae Rangers. Then there's the tabloid stories, My Booze Hell, and a' that shite. Supposedly kicks the bevvy, plays a couple ae seasons fur Dunfermline, then he's walked oot on them and jined Partick. Eventually turns up playin for Brora Rangers or some such bunch ae sheep shaggers. Fuck knows.

Another Great Shite Hope Ae Scottish Football doon the pan, eh. Pished away a' that talent, and expects us tae feel sorry for him.

Except he didnae. And except – and maist cunts forget this when they write aboot him – he was six years wi the Huns. Six years. Week in, week oot, he played brilliant for them, apart fae the very end. Except as well he got capped sixteen times. Shouldae been mair, like, but that's doon tae that balloon ae a manager we hud.

The Pars – three seasons, Partick – twa. Then I think he wis twa years wi Clyde afore he went sheepshaggin up north. Played a lot ae senior fitba for a pishheid. And a' through that time, he would dae magic oan the ba, and nae cunt ivver, ivver, said anyhin.

I mind seein him playin for the Huns in a European match on Sky wan night. Some bunch ae German basturts that were far tae guid for the Huns, eh. 4–3 doon on aggregate, and Tam gets the ba aff their star midfielder like sweeties aff a bairn and gans doon the inside right channel. And I'm stannin in this pub in Ferrytoon, and I'm shoutin at Laudrup, 'Make the run! Make the fuckin run!' Cause I can see where Tam wants tae play it, I can see it openin up.

So Laudrup makes the run, but the sweeper's right oan tae him, ken, Laudrup's left it tae late. So the ba goes out and the camera pans ontae Tam's pus, and he's got this expression, like, Ah cannae dae anyhin wi this cunt. Ah wis pishin masel laughin in this pub. Me and Brian Laudrup! Neither of us guid enough for Tam!

Did I get pished that night? I can just remember Tam scorin late oan wi wan o they blurry wans fae thirty yards tae equalise. Still went oot oan away goals though.

So, anyway, a' that's history, eh. Tam's finished playin' fur the sheepshaggers and the media's lost interest. But like a dug ayewis returns tae its ain boke, Tam turns up in the Ferrytoon Goth a couplae months ago. Where, for want ae somehin better tae dae noo the wife and weans have upped sticks, I'm haein a beer.

'Awright pal?' Tam strolls ower tae ma end ae the bar, pint ae Heavy in haund. Every cunt in the pub is watchin him, like, but nae cunt says anyhin. He looks me up and doon.

'Big cunt ae a sweeper, thon, eh?' He says. Like that game we played against Buckhyne Royal Albert fourteen year ago had been that eftirnin.

'Aye', I says, sookin on my pint. 'No a bad through ba, eh.' He's grinnin back at me, pretendin tae frown wi thae big beetle brows.

'No bad. No as guid as the three ye made a cunt ae afore that though.'

'Aye? Away and fuck, ya cunt ye.' I'm laughin, thinkin, fourteen year he's been playin senior, and he remembers some cunt that played wi him the once for Ferrytoon Juniors. Some boy.

He signals tae the barman, and gets ehs another pint, and one for himsel.

'No a bad finish, right enough,' he says. The scout fae the Huns wanted tae sign you up tae, but Ah said it was a fluke, like.

'Away and fuck,' I says again, punchin him oan the shoudir and laughin. 'Ah wish.'

He looks at me kind ae weird, like he's gonnae say somehin else aboot it, but the barman brings the pints ower and he's distracted. And eftir that, it's a command performance fae yer man, a' the stories he couldnae tell Hazel Irvine aboot his times wi the Huns, the Pars, a' the shaggin and drinkin. He is funny as fuck though. You can see the auld anes that clutter up the Goth lappin it up, pretendin no tae.

Six pints later and ma heid's spinnin. When Tam gaes aff tae the bogs I nip ootside and hae a boke, spatterin the lager ower the derelict shop site next door. The cauld air cuts intae me and I stop heavin. I feel a bit better, hae a couple ae gobs oan the grund and then straighten up fur a slash.

'Cannae hae the great Tam Johnston thinkin I cannae hold ma bevvy,' I say out loud, like ye dae when ye're pished. Talk tae yoursel, I mean.

'Ah ken ye cannae,' says Tam, ahent me. He's come oot eftir me. I can just make oot his shape at the edge ae the pavement.

'Awright, eh?' I say. I dinnae ken whit else tae say. Tae pished. I finish up ma slash and turn roond.

'You could see it, eh?'

'Whit?'

'When Ah did that hing wi the ba. No every cunt could, ye ken. That's hoo nae cunt ivver said anyhin.'

'That right, aye? Hoo did ye ken I could, Tam?'

He gave a kind ae shrug.

'Ah just kent. That game against Buckhyne. The wey ye looked at me eftir the free kick. Come oan, Ah want tae show ye somehin.'

Ma heid's reelin, partly fae the bevvy, partly fae whit's goin oan. Tam couldnae be a bufty, shurely, no wi a' thae birds he's shagged. If he is, he's probably strong enough tae... I pit the thought tae one side.

'Whit's that, Tam?'

'Come oan,' he says, headin up the Main Street fae the Goth. I huv tae hurry tae catch him up.

'Ever wonder hoo Ferrytoon's ca'd Ferrytoon when we're five mile fae the coast?' he says. He's chargin along past the playin fields at the auld Institute. It's dark. The lights seem tae hae gone oot in the toon ahead ae us.

'Eh?'

We're just at the first hoose in ma estate, or where I used tae live afore the wife gave me the heave ho. The Cooncil hooses loom large out ae the dark, black shapes seemin tae sook the darkness inwards. Tam's een are glintin in the dark. He wants an answer.

'Ehm...' I'm haein tae think ae somehin that'll satisfy the cunt. 'It's an auld word meanin somehin else?'

I can just make oot Tam noddin his heid.

'Clever boy. Come oan.'

He turns right at the first Cooncil hoose; there's a path there, half owergrown, which gaes up the wee hill ca'd Ferry Hill.

'It's Fairy Toon, F-A-I-R-Y.' Tam spells it oot for me, stottin up the path. Where is the cunt takin me? Has he fund magic mushies up here, or somehin? Me and ma brither never did, and we looked often enough.

'It was ca'd Fairy Toon eftir this hill, Fairy Hill. Ye heard ae fairy hills?'

'Aw aye.' I huv nae idea whit the cunt is oan aboot. His voice is getting kind ae muffled as we crash through a' the nettles and shite. I hurry up tae get closer.

'Fairy hills. Where fairies live. But the Scottish fairies werenae,' he corrects himself, 'arenae the poofy cunts like Peter Pan and a' that shite. As ye're aboot tae find oot.'

Ah'm gonnae meet the fairies. The cunt's away wi the fairies right enough, but ye can get that ECT fur that noo. I decide tae play along though, he might get even mair doolally if I laugh at him here.

He stops, and turns tae face me.

'Ah ken ye dinnae believe me. Ah ken Ah widnae. But then hoo did Ah get ma gift?'

He's staunin in the dark facin me, and then the moon comes oot fae ahent the clouds, and I can see his pus. He doesna look mental, staunin amongst the waist high nettles. Pished maybe. No mental. Aroond us, hings scutter aboot in the weeds and an owl goes past close by. Tam starts up.

'Come oan,' he says. 'They'll be waitin.'

And so they are. The fuckin fairies are waitin for us. Big, massive cunts they are, aboot seven fit tall, wi long, dark hair and oval een. They have long dark coats oan, but their wings stick oot their backs. The wings're as long as they're tall, but strang lookin, like the stuff they mak aeroplane bodies oot o. No wispy, poofy stuff.

The heid fairy's gien me the look.

'This him?' he asks Tam.

'Aye, that's the wan', says Tam, lookin nervous, like. The heid fairy's still gien me this look. I stert tae back awa, but twa ae the ithers huv come up ahent me – flown ahent me. I start fartin; arsehole's gaein like a wah-wah pedal. The heid bummer comes up tae me.

'Right you,' he says. 'You're claimed.'

They carry me tae this stane slab oan the tap ae the hill. The last hing I remember afore I pass oot is the pish runnin doon ma leg in a kind ae warm gush.

Next hing is I'm lyin oan tap ae the slab and Tam's bendin ower me.

'Come oan Goggsy. They've gone. Ah've passed ma gift oan tae ye.'

Ah stand slowly, tryin tae tak in whit he's said.

'Ah've passed it oan tae ye,' he says again. 'Ye've goat it noo, no me. Ye can dae magic wi the ba.'

Ma heid sterts tae clear, and I look up at the sky. The moon has disappeared again but ye can see some ae the stars. In ane o the hooses below the hill, a light gaes oan.

'Ya stupit basturt,' I say. 'Ya stupit fuckin basturt. Whit use is it tae me? I'm thirty year auld. Whit senior team's gaun tae sign a thirty year auld? Eh?'

'Heh-heh-heh-heh. *Exactly*. That's the point, Tam says,' laughin at me.

'Ya cunt ye,' I say, and go fur him.

Gift or nae gift he's quicker than me, though, and trips me up, followin up on top of ehs tae haud ehs doon. He leans closer tae me as if we'll be overheard, his breath stinkin ae Heavy.

'Ah'm no takin the pish, Goggsy,' he says, gently. 'Lissen – no, lissen tae me. Ah goat this gift when Ah wis fourteen, and it wis a curse. Sure it goat me playin fur Scotland, but it also made ehs intae an alky. Noo, Ah've been watchin ye. Had a coupl'ae tough brekks wi the wife and that. But ye're still gannin aboot like ye own the place. Look eftir yersel, play fives three times a week.' He laughs, 'That's whey ye couldnae haundle the bevvy. Ye're no a practised pishheid likesay me.'

He gaes oan. 'Noo, Ah could gie this gift oan tae some daft wee laddie like Ah wis, and he could pish it away like Ah did. Or Ah could gie it tae you, and ye could get back intae the Juniors. Lead by example. Let the daft wee laddies learn the hard wey, no the easy wey.'

I think aboot this, then nod, and he lets ehs up. I get ma breath back, and say, 'But Tam, ye could dae that yersel, bringin the kids oan and that. Couldn't ye?'

I look ower at him, but his heid's turnt awa fae me, lookin oot ower Ferrytoon.

'Naw Ah couldnae,' he says eventually. 'Even if Ah goat back in the team wi ma reputation, Ah'm no fit. Basturn doctor says Ah've goat cirrhosis ae the liver, like. Totally fucked.'

The wind seems tae drop, and Ah look ower at him. His heid's still turnt awa fae me. I dinnae ken whit tae say, so fur wance in ma life, I dinnae say nowt.

Tam looks ower at me.

'Haein the gift's no the main bit, ye ken. It's kennin ye hae it. It gies ye the confidence tae try anyhin. Confidence's the hing, man.'

'C'moan, Tam. It's getting cauld up here. I've goat some Bell's in the flat.'

He stots back doon through the nettles wi me, suddenly lookin auld and grey, like. I realise hoo much the gift has taken oot o him, and wonder when I huv tae pass it oan.

We walk past the recreation grund, still pitch black. I turn tae Tam.

'And nae cunt ivver said anyhin?'

Tam looks oot across the recreation grund, thinkin o a' the great games he's played in ower the years. Beside him, I'm still takin in whit it is he's gien ehs.

'Naw,' he says eventually. 'Nae cunt ivver, ivver said anyhin.'

Jesus Saves

Billy Cornwall

The captain
pats his shoulder,
'Wee Davy's
gonni take it.'

The ball dropped out of the sky, out of the wide blue heavens. It fell towards the mortal ground, mighty in its falling, and bounced at Wee Davy's feet. He looked at it, surprised. Normally, his luck was never this good.

Wee Davy glanced up. From nowhere, a cluster of defenders appeared, six feet tall, smelling like hell and charging straight towards him. Together, they blotted out the sun.

'I'm going to die,' he thought. 'Right now, at the tender age of 13, I'm going to be killed.'

But through the gathering darkness, through the wall of hairy opponents, a chink of light gleamed. An avenue, a path – he could see a bit of the goalpost. He hit the ball, a rising half-volley. It soared, it split the air, almost invisible, past the outstretched goalkeeper...

And battered off the woodwork, and behind for a goal kick. The others rounded on him.

'Ye missed it, ya tube!'

'What did ye no pass tae me for?'

And they turned away and trudged back up the slope, muttering.

Wee Davy gazed at the woodwork, its denial, the relieved goalie scampering after the ball. He looked up at the sky, the loitering clouds. From the goal kick, the ball went sailing by, half a mile up in the air.

This is unfair, Wee Davy thought. He had nearly scored, he had nearly... If Dalglish had been that close, if he had just about, almost but not quite scored...

The crowd roared in his head. *Hard Lines Dalglish!* they yelled. *Gaun Yirsel Wee Davy! That Wis Nearly...*

Heading back towards the halfway line, he again saw the ball soar by, punted in the other direction, pursued by a many-legged football beast. Dust and swear-words drifted down the breeze. He walked after the ball and the beast.

The game was going badly. They were losing and it was not his fault. The others were older and bigger. Mostly they were smellier too. They had picked him, Wee Davy was sure, just to make up the numbers in their team. And his lack of height and weight meant that he was having a pretty poor time of it.

Nobody would pass the ball to him. They were losing 19–1. He wanted to go home.

In the opposition goalmouth, a fight was in progress, boots flying everywhere, but after several ricochets and a few wild bounces, the ball scuttled out for a corner. Wee Davy stopped, glanced around.

The park was a wild green place, full of bushes and trees, and muddy bits of grass with goalposts on them. To the right, a path wandered off, occasionally peopled by ladies with pushchairs, choirs of little children trailing behind.

His team were getting gubbed, slaughtered. Also, they had a corner. What would Dalglish do, he thought to himself. Would he give up the ghost? Would he pack it in, wander off home, leave the game behind him?

He would if he was playing with these bastards.

But Dalglish has taken up position at the edge of the box. No-one has noticed him, no-one is marking him. One chance, he prays, just one wee chance...

The ball is thumped into the penalty area. Chest-high, it travels. A defender sticks out a despairing boot, misses it, the ball flies on towards Dalglish. He takes it on his chest, it bounces nicely in front of him, the crowd is going wild. *Last Chance, Last Chance* they yell. He spins, nips past one defender, past another, he lines up his shot. This is it, Dalglish must score, he draws back his leg – and Dalglish is clattered from behind and the ball sails off, wide of the target.

PENALTY, cries his side. AWAY TI FUCK, cries the other. THAT WIS NIVER A PENALTY. Dalglish is sprawled in the dirt, holding on to his leg. He writhes on the ground.

'Lookit that,' someone says. 'He's greetin!'

Sniffing, he climbs to his feet, gently tests his leg on the ground. A bruise is blossoming there, and his mother will surely kill him. He sniffs again, a manly sniff.

'Dalglish disni greet,' he mutters.

'What??'

But now sensation! A penalty has been awarded, and an opponent leaves the field, blood pishing from his nose and all down the front of his only good Hearts shirt. A penalty it is.

As someone scoots after the ball, Dalglish is dusted off by his captain, possibly the most ignorant shite for miles around. The captain pats his shoulder, 'Wee Davy's gonni take it.' The others are about to protest, but the captain has been known to cripple his own players, never mind the opposition, and the decision stands.

Mad Harry, the returner of the ball, waltzes up. Wee Davy takes the ball, places it carefully on the penalty spot. He looks towards the goalkeeper, standing poised on his line, a rather large chappie with yesteryears shorts on. He must weigh fourteen stone, and most of this goes out the way. Wee Davy steps back, measuring his paces. Just like Kenny Dalglish. This is it, he thinks to himself. One last chance. The only bloody chance! Something – anything. Jesus Saves, But Dalglish Nets The Rebound.

There ought to be a weight limit on goalkeepers.

He looks around, realises, everybody's looking at him. The park is almost silent, a few wee birds tweetering in far-off trees. The path beside the pitch is empty. We Davy wipes his hands on the back of his shorts, takes a deep breath. He runs towards the ball.

Heatherstone's Question

Des Dillon

they'd tip their hats and go
their separate ways, Matt and Pat
to meet the Celtic bus and Willie
to meet the Rangers bus

The two Heatherstone brothers, Pat and Matt had a farm on a hill in Galloway above the Doon O May. On a good day you could see Ireland were they supposed they must have come from sometime back in history. It was rocky land and apart from the three fields they had mostly sheep and a few old cows that seemed to be part of the family. None of them ever got married and even if Pat was ugly as sin Matt was a film star. You hardly ever seen them off the farm. Except for the Celtic games on a Saturday and Chapel on Sunday. Pat, probably cos of his ugliness, never spoke to nobody. Matt sometimes chatted but his head was always on the farm, always on what was to be done next. They both made sure all the work on the farm was done by Saturday so they could go to the games.

Sometimes Matt would need to borrow things. Diesel. Silage. Tools. Four times a year at most Matt would come down to Willie McGaw's farm to ask a favour. McGaw's farm was on better land. Not great but enough to make it more prosperous. Willie McGaw would look out the window at Matt moving down the hill step by step, bit by bit.

– Here's aul Matt coming, stick the kettle on. Willie McGaw would shout to Annie, Get the biscuits out.

Matt Heatherstone would chap the door, take a step back, and stand with his blue eyes pleading and his big hands clasped together. Like somebody holy. An overgrown alter boy. Willie would come out and not far behind him Annie with the tea and biscuits. Matt would stand at the door drinking the tea and rolling the biscuit over in his fingers, catching a glimpse now and then of the imposing kitchen table surrounded by who knows how many chairs. He never went inside the McGaw farmhouse. Never wanted to intrude. So he'd be chewing the cud all about the weather or the harvest. That's the way he was.

– Aye, mm mm, aye ye're right there sir right enough. Ye're right there so ye are. Willie would be going, nodding away at Matt.

It was the same every time Matt came down. He'd be an infinity nibbling and then come away with something like,

– Any chance of a lend of some diesel Willie? We've ran out.

Sometimes it was just a few slice of bread just that he wanted. Matt was shy and Willie respectful. So if he was wanting a loaf till the shops opened on Monday he might talk about his dogs for an hour and then ask for a few wee slices of bread to shove him into Monday.

– Ye couldn't see yer way to a couple of slice of bread to shove me an Pat into Monday Willie could ye?

And he'd get a loaf forever.

– Forget Monday cos bread's for sharin, Willie'd say.

Matt and Pat helped with muscle whenever he needed it. Through the years they helped, man and boy. Especially after all the McGaw boys, Rangers fans to a man, had left the farm for better things.

That's the way it went for years.

And years.

And years.

Every Saturday, at the bottom of the single track road, Matt and Pat would wish Willie good luck and he'd return the wish. They'd tip their hats and go their separate ways. Matt and Pat to meet the Celtic bus and Willie to meet the Rangers bus. By January 2001 Celtic were already running away with the league and Rangers were in a bit of a mess after a long time ruling Scottish football.

By February the snowdrops were up all over the hillside like white lace over green velvet. The blue sky soared overhead and the sun was orange in the morning and orange again in the evening. But this was the afternoon and the sun was yellow and oh so cold. There was a bit of a wind and the snowdrops' bowed heads were twisting uphill, straining in the gusts. Then falling back. Straining and falling back. Like they were watching Matt Heatherstone pressing through the Galloway winter. The wind was strong from the west and Matt could taste the Irish sea. Now and then the Mountains of Mourne appeared like history and were gone. Obscured by distant clouds. On he went, down the hill, his feet sinking through the gauze of snowdrops and rising; the leather flecked with pellets of water. As he stepped past the flowerheads seemed to be following the passing away of his boots as the wind flared up and died for a moment and their heads swung. Like they were admiring themselves because today Matt's boots were shining like mirrors. The snowdrops seen their whiteness transfigured in a moment's consciousness and – whoom – were left trembling in the waft of his boots, the earthquake of his soles.

He'd not been down for six months. Willie came out to meet him as usual and Matt stood at the gate talking about summer then falling quiet. Willie was wondering what he was wanting but said nothing. In the silence, the poetry of the morning curved over Heatherstone's eyes. Glistening. Brighter than usual. Matt stood on the path and spoke about autumn.

– Brings ye nothing but bad luck that, a wet Autumn, nothing but bad luck so it does.

Willie noticed there was something beneath Matt's words. The ever so ordinary words. Willie McGaw was moving backwards all the time, slow and imperceptible, but backwards just the same. By this time the tea had been handed out, and the biscuits. Backwards Willie McGaw was going all the time, sipping his tea and drawing Matt Heatherstone with him in the gravity of respect. Pulling him through the electromagnetic field of Matt's words still hanging in the air in front of his face, crisp and lovely like fog. Matt's wee words with greatness in them. Willie felt a mighty pang of sorrow, or grief, or something he'd not had since his sons started leaving. Here was a sudden and incredible empathy with Matt. He wished he could see more of this man, that they had been closer all the years they lived next to one and other. Then he realised they were at the door. The threshold that had never been crossed. Even if Matt was a Catholic and Willie a Protestant that was only half the reason the door had never been breached. They never knew what was in each other's houses. Till now. Heatherstone stood at the door and talked about winter, how it overlays the skin, flows into the lungs and burrows deep to the bones. Beneath his words of frost and ice was a shining coldness. A stillness. A clarity writers would die for.

– Will ye come in?

– I will, said Matt, for a wee minute.

It was only the snowdrops swinging in the wind with their heads bowed like reverence that witnessed Heatherstone from the top of the hill entering the inner sanctuary of the farm at the bottom of the hill. McGaw's Farm. Matt took off his cap and walked onto the alter of everyday life. Moved into the tabernacle of kitchen. A nod towards Annie as she said hello and turned away to save him awkwardness.

Matt sat at the fire looking mostly at the flames and wondering what they were. Flames? They leap from the dead peat, dance a crazy jig and then – there's nothing. Just a dark space where the flame used to be. A feeling that something is missing. Matt bent forward rubbing his hands, now and then holding them flat towards the fire even though he wasn't feeling the cold. Willie was in his rocking chair stuffing his pipe. Nothing was said. Nothing was said for a long time. It was only the sounds of Annie in the kitchen, the intermittent creak of the rocking chair and the lick of the fire as the flames sheened over the surface of their faces. And the tick of the clock. They were calm and they were patient. It might have seemed like a long time to you or me but sometimes we underestimate the peace that can be found in silence. We've lost the knowledge of the relativity of waiting.

And waiting.

And waiting.

But in Galloway, waiting is an art form. Every person a lesson in meditation. A contemplation. Life is oh so slow and so oh so sharp. One swallow soaring overhead in spring can be more memorable come December than the news item of the year.

After a while, Annie started making the dinner. Even before she said anything she'd laid three plates and set three places. There was ten chairs at the table but her family was up and away now. It knocked her out of kilter laying the other place for Matt when she was that used to laying for two. For her and Willie. But she done it, she laid three places because that's what you do. She'd often thought of the two places being reduced to one when Willie goes. If she went first Willie would eat on the hoof sitting in the rocking chair at the fire maybe. Aye, sitting in the rocking chair and filling his life with work and routine. The table would never be used again. But she never imagined three places again at this table. Not since Robert, their youngest son, went to London. Aye they came back and visited with their English wives and kids and strange stories of other places. But she'd never thought of an ordinary day and more than two at the

SINGING SOBB AN THE FUCK

66

ND

NG

HOPING

WASN'T

A DREAM

table. Not without the anticipation of visiting sons rippling through her like electricity. Not a Tuesday. A grey Tuesday with nothing remarkable about it and there she was laying three plates.

– Will ye take a bite? She went.

Willie raised an inviting eyebrow at Matt across the flagstones. Matt scanned the empty chairs before answering. His eyes stopped at every chair like he was looking for approval from the ghosts of their wandering children. He was an eternity before saying anything.

– Aye. I will.

So he was in there for the three courser. Soup. Steak. Apple pie. It was all served without speaking. The only sounds were the cracking of the fire and the squeaks of the old wood in Matt's chair. It had been a long time since it had borne weight. Now and then Willie McGaw and his wife exchanged polite puzzled glances. They didn't have a clue what Matt wanted.

And he was still there an hour after the dishes had been put back and the fire was banked up and the radio was soothing the night in. By then Matt and Willie were back in the chairs by the fire and Annie was polishing the vast table. Every knot, at some time or other, she had fixed her eyes on to get through arguments. Every grain her eyes had ran along to the laughter round the table; her wanes leaning back, cracking jokes and pointing at each other. The creases on their faces is what she remembered. But now the table was a surface of silence and edges where the lines drop off. Off into the world of space and shadows above the hardness of the floor. And she hoped none of her children would fall so hard they wouldn't be able to cry for help. Or so far they'd never be found. Or so deep nobody would hear their cries. That's all she hoped for; the rest she left in God's hands.

Back at the fireplace Willie had poured out two drinks.

– A wee somethin for yerself?

Matt searched for an answer in the flames.

– Aye. I will, he went, I will.

An hour later Matt was still there. He was still there and blinking hard every time the clock wound and chimed another quarter hour. Fighting sleep he was, and fighting something else too Willie noticed, fighting something else.

Willie wasn't an impatient man. He'd learned frustration won't bring the summer in or stop the beasts from dying. But it was getting late and nearly time for the Good Book. He didn't want to offend Matt by saying Protestant prayers in front of a Catholic. He had to know what Matt wanted. He made up his mind to ask. To give the big man an opening. It might be money. He's never asked for that before – money. That's what it'll be. And he's only too happy to give him some money. Hasn't he been his neighbour all these years. Never a bit of an argument or a dispute. Never a hint of bigotry. Always a nod and a touch of the cap when they crossed in opposite fields. And his brother Pat? Is he not a good God fearing Catholic? Aye. If it's money he wants he can have it.

– Another half?

– Aye... Aye...

And while Matt was drinking the other half Willie popped the question.

– So what'll be bringin ye here the night then Matthew?

– Ah, goes Matt, taking a sip, ah, now there's the thing. There's the thing right enough.

He took another sip and looked round the room. He looked round like he was looking for folks that might be listening. Or ghosts. He nodded over at the table where they had dinner hours before.

– I'm wonderin – ye couldny lend me a few chairs could ye?

Willie was puzzled. So was his wife. They thought it would be something bigger.

– Chairs? No problem, said Willie.

Matt finished off what he had in his glass.

– It's our Patrick, he's passed away like. I'll be needing the chairs for the wake, he said.

The fire flared up as the midnight wind crept in under the door.

The Saturday after the funeral Matt met Willie at the bottom of the single track road. They tipped their hats at each other, wished each other luck and went on their way. Matt to meet the Celtic Bus, Willie to meet the Rangers bus.

A Minute's Silence

Alan Bissett

It wis an act ae
aggression. Without sayin a
word, withoot firin a shot.

Aye.

Whit kin ah say, one day ye wake up an yer lifes been xactly the same for ten year. Ye look round the bar for the folk ye used tae ken, but ye dont see them, naw. Ken how? Thir no there. Theres jist these big long silences, like sighs. Like somebody sayin: this is it.

So. Me an the wife wentay rome this year, for the falkirk weekend, didnay wantay like! Rome ah says. Telt her: fuckin rome! Wer gawin, she says. Eywis wantit tae go, she says. Whit kin ye dae? English eh, the wife, an they dinnay hae that carry-oan doon there, they jist dinnay. Hows she tae ken! Shes no. An ye try an explain it tae her like, whit the score is like, but ye jist sound.... Stupits whit ye sound. Fuckin stupit man. So aye. Ah went.

That awright?

An see that vatican – ah ken ah ken, but its amazin like. Everybody should go at some point in their life eh. Ahm like dinnay dae this tae me hen. But shes like get yer arse in there. Thats me telt! But listen, ye get uptay thae doors right, an the heats bakin yer back, lashin yer sunburn man, an theres fuckin yanks shoutin, an japs wi thir cameras an nuns blessin themsels, an yer crushed up, crushed right beside them man, fuckin fuckin ahm like get me ootay here ah tell ye

But then.

Yer in.

Aye.

Size ae the place. Hits ye, this big blank silence like. Ah mind the light comin in, this fuckin shaftay... pure... like... an its coverin the whole flair coverin everythin man, the walls the statues the crosses aw man the wifes beside me, an shes talkin, talkin, sayin somethin man int it beautiful shes sayin, but im no hearin, no listenin, naw. Thought id never speak again in ma nelly puff, tellin ye. No a peep! Try it. Staun there. In that light. An listen tae nothin man nothin at aw xcept this long long silence.

Ringin oot.

An ken whit ah thought?

Ken who ah thought ae?

Danny.

Danny. Aye mind? Used tae call him the subbuteo kid. Naw? A tiny guy he wis, totesy, ah had tae look oot for the wee man so ah did, had tae dae aw his talkin for him, cos he wis shy. Danny! Aye ye widnay think it. Eyelashes like butterflies landin and hed bat them like that man total bat bat, like the whole world baffled him or somethin, which it proberly did. Just a wean like. Just weans, the two ae us. Even at the nursery though man, ah wis fightin for him, aulder ken? Four days. Four wee days eh, but it counts, like when wed be playin cowboys an indians an ah could force him tae to go the indian every time, an ken whit ahd dae? Ken whit ahd dae? Sayin pal, ken whit ahd dae? If we were playin quick-draw, ahd insist he hud tae reach intay his quiver for his arrow. Bang! Shoot him deid like, could never reach intay his quiver quick enough could he, naw. Weans eh! Cannay see shit go past them. Cannay even let a wee pal win wan game ae cowboys and indians. Hed go like that eeeeegh, make the chokin noises an like crumple intay a heap, deid like, then get up an blink thae eyelashes.

Can ah be the cowboy noo? hed go.

Naw, id go.

How no?

Cos ahm four days aulder than ye, id go

Bang!

Ach. Ah mean ah kent ah wis cheatin him like, an though partay me wis kinday ashamed ae masel, another partay me just wanted tae shoot him deid. Laddies though. Ye ken yersel.

Ach.

But like a pairay troosers so we were! Ye never saw the wan withoot the other, me and dan, aye ower the wids an up the trees man, climbin oot oantay the branches. Me giein dan a punty-up. Euch! Like that. He wis scared. A scared wee guy, so he wis, didnay like the heights. Get up there ya big jessie ahm like, cos once yer up there eh that big skys right above ye, pure blue man, an yer danglin ower the green bushes, the blue an the green, thats aw ye kin see, an yed go look at me ahm colt seevers man! Ahm the fall guy! Ih? No mind? Ahm the unknown stuntman, that made eastwood such a star. Whit age ye? Ach forget it then.

Anywey me and dan, total giein it that, ye think this is a cool stunt? Dae ye no think this is a cool stunt? Dae ye no think bein a stuntman wid be cool? An danny laughin, aye.

Danny laughin.

Man. Fuckin. We crammed the whole world intay that wee box thats a summers day, tell ye. Then hame for the orange juice, slurpin it up, ahl race ye! Ahl race ye! Go –

glugluglugluglug

Aw brilliant. Brilliant days. Ah wis first! Naw ah wis first! Aye so ye were. Right smart arse: ahl race ye round the block. You start at bobs shop an ahl start at the pakis an wel see who gets back here first, right go –

Oot on the bikes. Ye never go oot on the bikes? Aye wis it aw segas an nintendos for your lot? Well yed race right up tae the three steps at the end ae the street ken, the enday avon court. Theres these three steps an when we were wee, we cried them the three steps – cos ken theres three ae them – an yed rush uptay them man at the same time like that, pedals total gawin ten tae the dozen brrrrrrrdd. Crouched right intay the saddle like this, an wer like right? Ye ready? Ready? Wheels liftin aff the grund man like yer flyin total ET style. Intay the air, intay the bright blue yonder. Ah went higher! Naw ah went higher!

But eh.

Danny. Eh.

This wan time ah mind he hit the grund wrong. Scuds right across the concrete man. An ah jist mind the bike an danny makin this... weird... shape. Like ken, spokes an legs. Ken, metal an flesh. So ah runs ower tae him an there he is, lookin up at the sky, up at the sky man, wee gasps ech ech ech. And theres. This. Bone stickin ootfay his wrist.

Ahm serious like.
An ken whit he says? Ken whit he says? Ye listenin? He says
Telt ye ahd go higher than you.

Carried him hame. Airm round his shooder like, helps him tae his mams. Haud ontay me, ahm like, Ahl get ye there danny. An hes haudin ontay me wi his good airm an ahm like ye awright ye awright? An he looks up at me.

Son. Noo. Ah tell ye the thing wi danny: it wis thae eyes man. His look. Wis like at that moment, the pain. The bein pals. Everythin understood ken? Just.

Understood.

But then comes the fitba! Yabeauty it roars intae toon wan summer man, like a circus eh, an yer oot every night hard at it. Playin like the gemmes just been invented. The dark nights is yer foe. Ye ken yersel. Aye we were aw weans, we were aw weans.

See. Cos. Weans play a pure kind ae fitba. Aw this montay fuck ref an bawlin an rollin on the flair wi yer shins in her hauns, ye learn that. Ye learn it the wey ye learn tae greet tae get whit ye want. But pure fitba... its in the womb beside ye man. In the silence an calm. Its like...the sea or the desert or oxygen aw roond ye, the rhythm an glances an pattern ae the gemme ken? Ye feel it. That connection in a pass, reachin somebody across empty green space like...a message. A silent message.

Aye its only when fitba opens its fuckin big mooth it blows it.

Tell ye. Me an danny played pure fitba back then. Ahd promise masel that wee toerag widnay get past me like, but god help ye if ye took yer eye aff him for wan second, wan second man, an hed be gone, yed better believe it! Yed jist feel this wind – zhooom – whit wis that? Aw shit. Every goal yer cursin yersel but ken, beamin wi pride at dannys skills man. Yed stand back. Yed stand back an applaud.

Whit dae ye make ae that goal? hed gie it, Genius or jist brilliant?

An hed jog away like, an yed hae tae smile. Naw naw it wis awright, ye could take it, cos every goal – in a funny kinday wey – every goal wis for you tae.

Ma man dan.

But there wis this wan thing.

This wan wee thing.
Like a germ.

An it grows so slow ye dont notice.

Danny wis at st andrews an ah wis at hallglen primary. We lived in the same street like but went tae different schools. How can that be? Ahm jist a laddie an ahm thinkin how can that be? Same street different schools. Hm. See. Ye get folk who gie it that: fitbas a religion. Usually sayin it tae women giein it aye aye aye, its just some guys kickin a baw around, moan moan, which it is aye, nae gettin away fae that. But its the other thing tae. Two extremes. Two extremes ken. Ye pick a team. Ye pick a team when yer wee an it might be a choice based on nothin, arbitrary man, but think aboot whit it means tae the rest ae yer life. How holy it is. Whit ye daein aw that time xcept prayin? Whit ye daein xcept offerin up a piece ae yersel? Whits that word They yaise. Transubstantiation. Aye. Transubstantiation. When the spirit ae christ comes doon fae heaven.

Ah ken. Listen tae it! But like fitbas a mystery eh. Its aw in the glances, the breathin, the beatin ae yer heart; thats whaur it lives. Somethin tae dae wi bein alive. Mortal. Its no scarfs and fuckin badges thats for sure.

So same streets different schools. It wis that craig eadie who answered the question like, ken craig? Naw. Well baw-heided eadie we used tae caw him. His faither wis jailed a few year ago for a fight the night ae that omagh bomb. Went intae wan ae Their pubs an demanded tae ken who done it. Thats the eadies.

His laddie wis the same like, wan ae these smart-arses whid go up and doon the dinner queue askin folk if they had a 'pencil' or a 'sharpener'. Ah ken. Weans. An yel mind there wis eywis wan lassie whid say she had a pencil or a boy whid say he had a sharpener, well eadie wid laugh an point like, an even though they wurnay sure whit the hell pencils and sharpeners had tae dae wi anythin, the whole queue wid laugh. So eadie gets roundtay me wan dinner time, an hes like

Have ye got a car or a garage?

A car.

Have ye got a rubber or a ruler?

A ruler.

Are ye a tim or a hun?

This wis a new wan. Ah hesitates. Fatal. He goes

Ma faither says tims spread lies and nits, an ahm no eatin dinner next tae somebody wi nits!

Ah wis just tryin tae work oot if a tim wis sharpener-shaped or no.

Whits the difference? ah says.

If ye go tae chapel yer a tim. If ye go tae sunday school yer a hun.

That didnay clear it up like. Ah wis pretty sure ahd never been tae a chapel, but then ahd only been tae sunday school the twice. It wis the maist borin thing oot man. They just sat and talked tae ye aboot jesus an banged on aboot how we should aw love wan ither. So ah telt him ah wis a hun jist cos ah didnay want him thinkin ah had nits.

An soon ye jist kent.

Jonesy: hun. Donovan: tim. Dek allison: hun. Danny

An like ah say. It grows so slow ye dont notice.

Me an danny though! Wed be oot at the crack ae dawn every weekend. First thing in the mornin ahm chappin his door, bouncin the baw, chewin the gum like. Wed go tae the lock-ups at the enday avon court an practice penalties. Whos takin this wan? Davie cooper. Cooper steps up, shoots. And hes missed! Coopers missed! Who's takin this wan? Brian mcclair. Mcclair has to score...

Folk just gettin oot their beds on a setirday an theres two weans takin penalties ootside, smashin them against the lock-ups. The abuse we got man! Ah mind one time this guy started shoutin at us - get tae fuck away fae there and play at yer ain bit! Eight in the bloody mornin! Tell ye whit though, some cheek on the boy danny. Hed done a bit growin up since the nursery like, wis only a couple ae year away that danny wid be scared ae naebody. He gies it that, aye up yours, an flicks the baw ontay the enday his fit, lobbin it at the guys winday. The guy ducks away like, an danny starts laughin at him, the feart look on his face. Funny as fuck. But then he sees dannys top an goes apeshit man, shoutin an swearin, things ah didnay ken the meanin ae at the time. Words that felt like spit landin: papish. Chinese words like wee feen yin. Even folks names: ya mick.

Two minutes later dannys faithers at the door. Cawin him an orange bastard.

Ah mean the guy had a fairly bad tan but ah widnay have went so far as tae caw him orange! Fist here, doof, blooter there, boof, then the guys wife screamin an tryin tae pull them apart an dannys faither stormin right at us, face total like that grrrrrr. Sees ma top.

In, he says tae danny.

Dans like dad dad, whit-

In!

An then theyre away, danny dragged behind him like this wee green an white accessory. Wisnay allowed tae see me for weeks eftir that. Ah played wi the weans fae ma school and danny played wi his.

Big long summer between us.

Aye. It wis then the fitba started gettin mair serious. Gradually like. But before ye ken it yer comin hame an yev lost an ye feel this rage, this rage at the surface ae yer skin.

Danny hated the losin tae. Ask anybody. Setirday, eftir the fitba, if They won and we didnay hed be straight roond tae yer hoose, an yer mam wid make excuses for why ye couldnay come tae the door. If we won and They lost, itd be his door. His mam.

Ah mind the day They signed mo johnston. Mam hudnay read the paper like, an she let him in. Fucksake she let him in! Danny chargin up the stairs, man ah couldnay face it - ah ran tae the toilet an locked the door. Total sittin there heid in ma hauns, starin doon at the rug while danny stands in the hall singin mo mo super mo, super maurice johnston!

Two months later ahm bangin on his door singin the xact same song.

Noo. Souness had mccoist and hateley in the same frontline, whit wis he needin mojo for? Think aboot it. He widnay have bothered his arse if They hadnay tried tae sign him first. Tell ye pal, it wis an act ae agression. Withoot sayin a word, withoot firin a shot. Fuck you in sign-language.

Just like danny blessin himsel. Runnin past eftir scorin a goal like, makin the sign ae the cross or kissin the wee crucifix on his chain, peter grant style. Mind peter grant? Played for Them? Ach yer too young. Well there wis not one player ae Theirs ah hated mair than peter grant. Didnay mind paul mcstay, didnay mind roy aitken – didnay really like them right enough but ah didnay mind them either. But that grant. Fuck. Wi the blessin himsel, the crossin himsel, the blatant papishness. Aye he kent. An when danny did it, well whit kin ah say. It gave the gemmes a wee edge.

Is that really necessary? ahd go, an danny wid jist shrug like that. Whits it got tae dae wi the gemme? ahd say.

Whits the union jack got tae dae wi the gemme? hed say. Plenty rangers fans wavin it on setirday.

True enough like. Ma uncle david had this union jack on his waw an a picture ae the queen there on the mantelpiece. Never gied it much thought eh til wan hogmanay ma faither starts singin flower ae scotlan, an david turns an gies him this look.

Hey, david goes. Quit it wi the rebel songs.

Rebel songs? goes ma faither, Flower ae scotlan?

Aye, david says. Send them homewards tae think again? Thats the royal forces yer referin tae.

Ah ken ah ken. Some folk eh? Well ah telt danny the story, whit dae ye make ae that? ah says. Flower ae scotlan a rebel song!

Danny didnay say anythin. We were watchin the auld firm cup final like, mind the wan wee joe miller scored? Fae a crap gary stevens passback? Anyway half-time ah comes in wi the juice an danny goes

Ahm no drinkin that.

How no?

Cos its orange, he says.

Ah looks at the gless.
Its fuckin um bungo!
Ahm no drinkin it, he says.
Ah looks at the gless again.
But its fuckin....um bungo!
Aye well, he goes, an turns back tae the fitba. Ah dinnay like it any mair.

Aye pal.
If ye can see whaur this is gawin yev been there.

Whit? When wis the last time ah spoketay him? Gid question. Let me see noo, the last time ah exchanged words wi danny ah think...we were still at the school.

Aye. It wis an inter-schools gemme, falkirk high against st mungos. Some fuckin gemmes like, legendary, ask any ae this lot. But the thing is, even though yed kent the guys in the other team for years, had even played in sides wi them, it wis different. They were a team fullay papes.

Noo thisll sound daft, but ken the way ye become...usedtay a lassie. So that eftir a few times ye can predict the things shel dae? In bed like? Theres a soraty eh language ye dinnay hae tae speak, thats in the the wey yer bodies fit thegither. Then mibbe one time she dis somethin oot the ordinary, an it gets ye thinkin. Wonderin. Whits she uptay? Whys she chainged?

Well dannys style wis different that day. The wey he played the gemme: he barged past an ah felt the sharp bone ae his elba for the first time eh. So ah went intae the tackle wi ma studs up. Next thing ah find masel markin him an hes cawin me an orange bastard an ahm cawin him a fenian cunt an ahm spittin in his face.

He wipes it aff an ah dinnay recognise the look in his eyes.

So.
Thae four days between us became ten year.

Whit? Aw aye, still saw him aboot like. Sometimes hed be in the pub, singin songs ah didnay want tae hear wi guys ah didnay want tae ken, but eftir the stabbin –

Eh? No mind? Wis in aw the papers. Couplay year ago: wan ae Them stabbed oan the twelfth ae july? Well, eftir that ah tried tae mind the last time ahd seen danny.

He wis waitin for the bus tae take him tae a gemme. Staunin drinkin lager in the sun like, starin up at the sky. Same as that time he crashed his bike an ah took care ae him. Mind ah telt ye pal? Aboot his eyes? Well he looks ower at me and he looks away again, as if hes never seen me afore.

It wis.

Understood.

Aye though that vatican. Whit a place. Somethin aboot it though ye cannay quite get yer heid round, less yer wan ae Them, but ah tell ye: its there. Ye feel it. In the quiet like. In the dark. Somethin...sacred. Somethin judgin ye.

Ach ah dinnay ken, but its like when they had that minutes silence for danny at parkheid, an aw the players had their heids bowed, an aw the crowd did tae, an it wis silent, like a communion or a prayer or somethin Tell ye, when i came oot that vatican ah was greetin so ah wis. Big huge tears man jist rollin aff the face.

Telt ye ahd go higher than you, he says tae me.

An ken whit? The wee cunt did.

Sure pal, if yer buyin likes.

For the rangers!

Aye.

The Bigot

Denise Mina

the city breathed out an ooh
of disappointment, a grieving
coo for the almost-goal

Big Alec didn't like women. They all knew it and yet Jonno had brought her to sit at the side of the room and listen in on their conversation. She was pretty, a small, slim blonde thing with opal skin and candy floss hair. She had strappy shoes on, red patent leather criss-crossed over her scarlet painted toes and her dress was artery red, a deep, dark red that made Jonno's mouth water when he looked at her. She kept her eyes down and sat on the long leather settee at the side, cradling a fat wee dog in her arms. The dog was so ugly its face looked inside out, silver trails dribbled from its nostrils and an obscenely pink tongue lolled from the side of its mouth.

'Wit is that doing here?' said Big Alec.

Jonno smiled nervously,

'It's just a wee dug, Mr Wilson...'

'I didn't mean the dug. Wit is *that* doing here?'

The blonde didn't flinch. She stood up, dropped the wee dog to the floor and unravelled a red leash that matched her dress and shoes. She walked out of the door, tugging at the collar. The tiny monster shook its head, sending a shiver rolling through the rolls of fat on its back, and followed her out of the room.

Big Alec didn't speak. He simply looked from the space she had occupied to Jonno and back again.

'Sorry,' whispered Jonno. He'd meant to impress them, ignorant of the horrible true history of Lindsay, the ex-Mrs Big Alec, and the teacher from the pottery class. It was a mistake, a miscalculation at a meeting where every decimal point would count.

They were all there right on time, dressed smart, despite where they were going onto afterwards. Ali Bax was dressed in a shiny grey suit, Pat the Tank had a black suit on and Nick and Jonno both had blue on, unafraid of being caught after the game in the wrong colour. It was Big Alec's house and he was the only one without a suit on. Alec wasn't Big but he was broad. Fat actually, like the girl's dog. His skin was sallow and his hair an unnatural midnight black, thick with wet-look gel. He liked to tramp around the house in the new Ranger's away kit and today, because of the match, was wearing Rangers slippers and a scarf as well. It made him seem terrifyingly uncompromising, thought Pat the Tank. It was belligerent to have worn such an outfit for mixed company.

They were in a room at the back of the house. It had a huge oak table in the centre with ten chairs set comfortably around it. One wall was covered in wooden panelling and against the other wall sat a ten foot long black leather settee with chrome legs.

'Nice,' said Ali Bax standing at the window, taking in the view. 'It's nice here.'

Outside the window a sunny immaculate lawn rolled downhill to a mini driving range and the electric blue edge of an artificial lake. At the bottom of the lake, in a forest of green hair, sat a Merc SLK 2.3 convertible with Lindsay and the teacher from the pottery class strapped in the front seats. Three years on the superior beige leather upholstery was badly discoloured from cradling rotting flesh. Lovers' pact suicide, Big Alec would say if they ever asked. He'd reported them missing and everything.

'Let's get on,' said Pat The Tank.

The Old Firm kick off was in ten minutes and they didn't want to watch it together. Big Alec had already wasted thirty minutes on a guided tour around the house, showing them the jacuzzi, the billiard room, kitchen, jacuzzi, lounge, TV room, lounge, jacuzzi. Pat didn't know if it was the same jacuzzi or three different ones because all the rooms looked the same, the same yellow walls and beige shag pile, the same black and grey furniture, same big ugly ornaments lit up on the glass shelves. Alec had wasted so much time that they were going to miss the kick off. Pat and Jonno both had tickets for the game.

'See,' Big Alec was still staring at Jonno, 'I don't like women being in on my business because of something that happened.'

Pat the Tank caught himself sighing and slowed it down into a deep breath. Why had they agreed to divvy up today? Today of all days.

'My wife,' continued Alec, circling the table to Jonno's side, 'My wife robbed me and ran away with a guy. Filled her bag full of readies and left. No note, no nothing. How do you think that made me feel?'

Jonno looked at the others for a clue but found nothing on their faces. It was his first carve up, his first big meeting and he was

HE ALWAYS GOT

BLAM

WE

WHICH

WAS FAI

COS HE WAS S

P 184

ED

OR ANY GOALS

LOST

ENOUGH,

ITE.

completely out of his depth.

'It made me feel BAD,' said Alec turning pink, his wet look black hair trembling at the gelled tips, 'Very *REJECTED*.'

Pat smiled at his trainers. Alec was good but he could be a bit obvious sometimes. He was toying with the boy, showing the rest of them he still had it in him, sending them a warning before the start of the game.

'Women,' he said, 'Are sneaky. They can't be trusted with anything, no matter how small. They'll turn on ye and grass ye and steal your wallet on the way out.' He leaned in tight to Jonno's face, poking at his nose with fat finger, 'Never forget and never talk business in front of them.'

Jonno nodded, his mouth hanging open slightly. Pat realised that Alec was wasting time deliberately and he suddenly understood why the meet had been called for now. Everyone would be jittery, everyone wanting out so they could go and watch their team in peace. Four hundred grand was a lot of money, even for a man like Alec.

'Alec,' said Jonno, thrown on the back foot, 'I didn't mean to offend ye.'

'Well,' Alec narrowed his mouth and reared up, 'Ye have offended me.'

Across the room Ali Bax snickered and Alec lost concentration, forgot himself and smiled. The guys around the table smiled and laughed and Alec turned to them,

'Fuck yees,' he grinned. 'You fucking ruined that.'

Bewildered by the rapidly shifting atmosphere, Jonno half-smiled.

'Come on,' said Pat, to him 'Let's sit down and do it. I've got an appointment this afternoon.'

Ali and Nick nodded over at him, Nick running his tongue along his lower lip.

'So have we.'

Alec touched a wooden panel at the side of the room, tripping a mechanism that slid two opposing doors open slowly to reveal a mirrored bar with crystal decanters. The dark room filled with white deflected light. Built into the doors were sliver shelving units holding every kind of glass. Alec pointed a thick finger at Jonno, flicking back to the bar,

'Glenmorangie,' he said, 'No ice.'

Jonno paused for a heart beat before stepping around to the bar. The other men had called their drinks out and before he even realised what had happened, Jonno had gone from a player to the barman. Alec took out a long cigar and sat it on the table in front of him like a dessert spoon.

'This is what I propose: Fifteen percent to Ali and his team. Twenty per cent to Nick,' he nodded politely at Pat, 'Five extra for his cars.' Pat nodded back. 'Thirty to Pat and thirty five to myself.'

Jonno, delivering the malt, flinched and dropped the heavy crystal glass onto the table.

'COASTER,' said Alec, 'Ya ignorant prick. Where were you brought up, Barlinnie?'

Jonno stared at him,

'Am I getting nothing?' he said quietly.

Alec took a slug of his whiskey and looked around the table.

'I did my bit,' said Jonno, 'Am I getting nothing?'

Alec looked him up and down,

'I don't feel like giving this prick anything.'

'But it was my idea...' said Jonno, backing off around the table to Pat's side, looking for allies.

'Ahh, come on,' said Nick, 'He did his bit, give him his cut.'

'D'you want to give him a cut?'

'Aye,' said Nick

'Give him some of yours, well.' He said, a smile hidden far behind his eyes. Pat could tell that Alec had planned this. He'd been planning this since the beginning.

'If,' said Pat slowly, 'We don't pay Jonno anything,' Jonno twitched nervously and Pat put a calming hand on the table in front of him. 'Will anyone else ever come to us?'

The other men nodded their assent.

'Come on, Alec,' said Pat, 'Give him his place.'

Big Alec finished his drink, pushing the glass across the table towards Jonno with his fingertips,

'Can ye remember what was in this glass?' he said.

'Aye,' nodded Jonno quietly.

'Well, fill it up then.'

Jonno looked at Alec for a moment. A fat red-faced man in a ranger top and scarf, laughing at him. As far as Alec knew Jonno'd set the whole thing up and yet he wasn't going to give him anything. Jonno hadn't set it up at all. Anne Marie, the blonde in the red dress, had the idea. She told him to approach Pat and get Alec in on it, but they didn't know that. Alex flexed his middle finger and pushed the glass a millimetre towards him. Jonno was faster than the fat man. In a second he'd leaned down, pulled a knife from his sock and threw himself across the highly polished table, but he skidded on the slippery surface, spinning at a ludicrous angle so his hip ended up where he meant his head to be. The seated men leapt back from the table and Pat the Tank was on Jonno, holding his legs steady while Alec hit him on the back of his head with the heavy glass. His last thought was for little Anne Marie, unprotected and alone in a house full of dangerous, murderous men.

The back of Jonno's head was a bloody matted mess, his leg twitched as a slick of dark blood spread urgently across the sleak table. Panting and disgusted, Pat let go of the boy's legs. His face was freckled red, his sharp suit ruined. He looked at his hands and screamed.

'The match starts in four minutes.' He said, *'Four minutes.'*

Fighting for breath, Alec smiled and stepped back to the bar, reaching into it. Nick and Ali ducked inadvertently, embarrassed when they saw him draw a remote control out from the side of the bottles. He raised his hand over the warm body of Jonno and pressed a button. On the same wall as the bar a wooden panel slid soundlessly behind its neighbour, revealing a wide screen plasma television. Pat sagged, 'I didn't want...'

Alec grinned at him, lighting up the cigar, 'What? What didn't ye want?'

Exhausted, Pat shook his head. What could he say? He didn't want to watch it with a fucking psycho Hun bastard?

'Nothing,' he said, waving Alec away, 'nothing.'

Suddenly, blood splattered noisily off the table and onto the floor, pooling in a viscose puddle, ruining the carpet.

'Do we need to watch it in here?' said Ali quietly.

'Oh,' said Alec indignantly, 'What's wrong? Is there not enough booze for ye here? Not enough seats? D'ye not like my house?'

Pat and Nick looked at each other.

'Right,' said Nick, 'But we'll carve it up right after?'

Pat nodded,

'The minute the full time whistle goes, we'll sort this out, right?'

'Guys, guys,' Big Alec opened his arms wide and fell back onto the black leather settee, 'What's your hurry?'

There was ten minutes left before injury time and they were all wishing they were somewhere else, all wanting to get the fuck away from Alec. It was the least Pat had enjoyed an old firm match since he was a wee fella. It had been a tense nil-nil draw and they couldn't shout or cheer or display any emotion because Alec was battered on Glenmorangie and had already punched Nick in the mouth for saying that Alex McLeish wouldn't see the end of the season. Jonno's body lay face down on the table, occasionally letting off burps or farts but mostly lying still, dripping onto the shag pile. Pat could see now that Alec'd planned the whole thing, organising the day so that they would be exhausted and compliant and desperate to get away from him by the time the divvy came. The trick, he reminded himself, was to stay calm and not let it cloud his judgement. The worry was that Alec would pull some other stunt before the end.

'Ho,' said Alec, slurring and pulling himself up from a slouch, 'Where the fuck is she?'

Ali Bax looked at him, nervous and exhausted,

'Wha'?'

'Where's she? The woman he brought with him. The red woman.'

The men looked at each other warily.

'She's loose in my house,' said Alec, standing up and falling slightly to the side. He pointed at Nick who was dabbing his sore mouth, 'You find her.'

'Aww,' groaned Nick, 'There's eight minutes to go.'

Alec bent down and leaned his big hands on Nick's knees, speaking so close into his forehead that Nick could feel his breath on the skin,

'Find that fucking hole,' he said.

'Come on Mr Tingle,' said Anne Marie, tugging the wee dog's leash. The dog sat down on the tarmac and looked away from her. He was panting heavily and his tongue was as far out of his mouth as it would go. He had walked for ten minutes and couldn't go on. She muttered 'pete's sake' under her breath and bunny-dipped down to him, scooping him up in her free arm. In the other she carried a vase, green with gold trim, a disgusting ornament from one of the illuminated shelves in the back lounge.

'You'll make me drop this lovely vase, Mr Tingle, yes you will, you bad, bad wee doggie-dog.'

She wanted it the moment she saw it on the tour. She didn't suppose for a moment that Alec remembered it was Lindsay's vase, that their Mum had given it to her because she was the eldest. He probably thought it came with the house. She walked across to the four by four and put Mr Tingle down, taking the retractable ruler out of her pocket. Jonno wouldn't mind about the car, she decided, someone would drive him home. She jimmied the door open and slid into the front seat,

'Come on Mr Tingle,' she leaned out, holding out an open hand for the fat dog to sit his belly in and lifted him into the passenger seat. 'You mind that nice vase,' she said sitting it next to him on the chair.

Partick was deserted. She passed small girls and occasional women walking down the road or standing listless in the sunshine, watching dogs that may or may not have belonged to them. There were no cars. Suddenly, from open windows in houses and flats, the city breathed out an 'ooh' of disappointment, a grieving coo for the almost-goal. Not one single other car passed by as she took the slip road.

The motorway was empty as well. She took her eyes off the road for just a moment as she came through the tunnel and looked down on a big grey estate under the lip of the flyover. A tiny girl in a pink dress skipped slowly across the broad dual carriageway, followed by a panting Alsatian dog. It was like a dream, so quiet and calm, as if the city wanted her to get away. She'd go to London, and then Spain maybe. Or Malta, somewhere they spoke English. Somewhere hot. Lindsay always loved hot places. They went on holiday to Malta together before the fall out, before she met and married Alec Wilson. They were making friends again and had met, once for lunch and once at the house, just before Lindsay went missing forever.

'Gone?'

'Aye,' said Nick, shuffling at the door, trying to see the screen past Alec's head, 'Couldn't see her anywhere and then we looked out and saw the Shogun was gone out the front.'

Alec turned and looked at Jonno's corpse on the table.

'She took his car?' He turned to the company, 'She knows he's been popped.'

'Wait a minute, I saw him...' Pat stood up and checked Jonno's pockets, 'Look,' he said, holding up a key and remote button, 'How did she get into it?'

The men looked at each other and their faces fell. Ali Bax stated the terrifyingly obvious,

'She's a crim,' he whispered.

Big Alec went into the master bedroom alone and came out ashen faced and missing a Rangers slipper.

'How could she know?' He said, repeating himself over and over, 'How could she know where I kept it?'

'Where's she gone?' said Nick.

'Where would anyone go with four hundred grand of our money?' said Pat. 'She's gone to the fucking airport.'

The woman was wearing a uniform and a little hat but she wasn't an airhostess. If she was an airhostess she'd be on an aeroplane, surely.

'And when will you be travelling?'

Anne Marie tapped her red finger nail on the high desk.

'Now,' she said and giggled.

The woman looked at her curiously,

'Do you have any hand luggage?'

'No, just this,' she held up the ugly green vase, 'I think it's worth a lot of money.'

The uniformed lady smiled and glanced at her screen.

'There's a flight in twenty minutes to London Heathrow.'

'Okay,' the blonde put her hand into the vase and pulled out a fistful of fifty pound notes.

'It only costs two hundred and thirty,' said the uniformed lady, staring at the bundle.

'Oh,' Anne Marie counted out two hundred and fifty and shoved the rest of the notes back in. It was then that the uniformed woman noticed the leash on her wrist. She followed the scarlet ribbon to the fat little dog on the ground.

'I'm afraid you'd have to book if you want to bring the dog on board.'

'Oh, well,' smiled the blonde, 'I'll sit him on my knee.'

'This isn't the bus,' said the woman impatiently.

'He won't bother anyone,' pleaded Anne Marie, 'He's a nice wee dog.'

The woman sneered at her with draw string lips.

'You can either leave the dog or I'm afraid I can't sell you the ticket.'

The entire capacity of Ibrox stadium was swarming through Govan, blocking all the roads. Coaches of drunk men sang and waved out of the windows as they waited patiently to get onto slip roads to the tunnel, clogging the city's arteries. On the motorway flyover Nick edged the car slowly forwards. The queue for the cut-off snaked along the road for a mile. Below them the dual carriageway was a river of blue bodies and slow moving cars.

'FUCK,' bellowed Big Alec, red and ridiculous in his football kit. He raised a slippered foot and kicked the back of Nick's seat so hard Nick could feel the reverberation through to his knees. 'FUCK.'

Back outside Anne Marie knelt down and patted the wee dog's head. He panted, the rolls of fat on his chest heaving as he tried to catch his breath. She stood up, scooping her toe under his little bum and pushing him towards the strip of lawn in front of the hotel.

'Go on,' she said under her breath, 'Fuck off.'

The dog sat down and looked over its shoulder at her. Anne Marie swivelled on her heels and walked steadily back to the airport doors, clip-clopping her high heels against the concrete, slapping the airline ticket against her leg.

Sufisticated Football

Suhayl Saadi

perhaps it was the Soccer Satan,
the relegated angel

One midsummer's night, awhile back, I was lying in the cells at the dark bottom of the Old Partick Police Station. It was the balmiest night I can remember, perhaps because I was tanked-up on Supers and a whiff of crack, to boot. But just before I had arrived at this spot, someone had given me a small square of card, on which was emblazoned a tiny, monochrome figure clad in the 1882 soccer strip of Pantelleria's First Eleven. Well, to be honest, their only Eleven. And since, at this point, we're into truth (the whole, and nothing but), then I may as well admit that the reason I was there that night was because I had been attempting to play football on the roof of a four-storey Glasgow tenement while listening to a hundred watt rendition of *The Living is Easy*, an old number from the Dream Police. An interesting para-gravitational experiment. That's what happens when you ingest small sections of cardboard in your evening porridge. You see, I had spent years writing around, commentating on and thinking about football, and I had come to loathe the voyeur which I had become. So that was why, on that burning, midsummer's eve, I had accepted the offer of a dance with the various substances of the night.

I was lying on the hard stone floor and my belt and laces had been removed. My eyelids were bruised, possibly from an encounter with the men-in-black, or was it the boys-in-blue? Anyway...

Through the bars of the high window of my cell, I could just make out the crescentic spine of the moon and beyond that, a blackness which was inordinately deep. It seemed odd that there should've been no stars when an entire slice of moon was visible. I allowed my tender lids to close. A breeze flitted across the swollen skin and this should have soothed me, yet it caused panic to wind like a spring inside my chest and so, painfully, I opened my eyes again.

Facing me, sitting cross-legged on the floor, was the astral body of Akbar Allegro. I knew it was his astral form because, in places, I could see right through the red football top, straight through his ribs, heart and spine to the hard stone wall. He was smiling. I recognised him from the archaic mini-discs my father used to play. Old Akbar was balding and grey'd and crow's feet had already begun to stagger along the skin towards his temples.

How did you get in? I asked, aware that my voice seemed to be coming from the end of a long tunnel.

He shrugged.

Through the bars. How d'you think?

I chuckled.

You always were a sleek one.

So they said.

Midfield, wasn't it?

I didn't really have a position. After a while, I would go to wherever the ball drew me.

Like a magnet.

A bird.

I sucked in my breath.

So, Akbar, what brings you all this way through the night air from the clean blue line of the Riviera to the wondrous smoke-stacks of the dear green prison?

I came to see you, you dolt!

Now it was the great midfielder's turn to pause.

Well, what are you waiting for?

I reached into the lining of my jacket and with a sense of triumph I pulled out a miniscule notepad and a boot stud biro. Being a sports journo meant that I was always prepared.

I... I'm ready, I said.

Akbar Allegro stretched his spine, puffed out his chest and inhaled deeply and this action caused some of the night to tauten around his form, so that he grew more solid than before. His scarlet shirt and yellow shorts-and-socks glowed in the moonlight as though he were standing along the halfway line of a football pitch, waiting for the kick-off whistle and dreaming of the perfect fractal. Then his form began to alter again, red-and-yellow-and-black re-arranging themselves like in an interactive hologram, only more. Then I realised that he was singing his body into shape and the red, yellow and black, took the form of letters, thus:

GHOSHT

I tried to scribble it down in longhand, but my pen had run out of ink. I shook it vigorously, swore in three dialects and then sucked hard on the hollow end. Almost gagged on the foul blue chemical taste.

By then, then his whole body had become a mouth and the mouth began to speak:

A football game is a reflection of the cosmos and the cosmos is a reflection of love.

Ghosht is the Urdu word for 'meat'. The physicality of things is the meat of the Game. A bum pass sounds like the word, ghosht – especially in Scotland, where the ball is often sodden. The players move through glue around the pitch, there are obstacles at every turn. Even if you stand still, someone else is gonna come and get you, take the ball off you, propel you inelegantly back into the void. Tackles, tentacles, fish. Our lives are the ghosts of our selves. The ball itself is meat. Bull leather. And yet, it is fashioned in the form of a perfect sphere. It is insufflated, not with blood, but with breath. Breath, moving across darkness, becomes the Word. Like you and I, Ghosht strives to be more than itself, to lift and stretch its reality, and the realities of a million spectators, all of whom become instant birds, ersatz judges. A parliament of fish and fowl.

I awoke and it was dawn in the Police Station. First light hovered tremulously beyond the bars. I was lying curled-up on the floor but I wasn't the least bit cold. I thought of my life in the chabolas, of the family I had never had, of the dusks and the dawns and the feel of the sun searing into my back as I touted around the alleyways for money. And I decided that it really hadn't been worth it. Why had I been born into the life of Acebo, the street-kid? What had been the purpose? What was the game? My body felt stiff. My skeleton was fifteen years old, yet I felt as though I had aged decades during the night. I was slumped, naked, in the midst of thirty similar unfortunates and we were all lying in pools of urine, which had coalesced to form one great stinking lake. I was the only one awake. I had not slept all night.

With a loud, iron clanging, three soldiers entered and the first seams of daylight slunk in behind them. The soldiers had to stoop to avoid striking their skulls on the concrete ceiling and they clambered awkwardly in their studded boots over bodies and piles of excreta. They grabbed me roughly by the arms and neck. My legs promptly gave way. I could taste their breath on my face. They were expressionless.

The light outside was pure and blinding and it burned into every pore. After six weeks in the low cell, I had become a worm, half-blind and crawling around on my belly. Even though it was barely dawn, any light whatsoever had become intolerable.

They dragged me to a piece of waste ground which was surrounded by a circular, eight-foot high wall of corrugated zinc. I felt the coarse, metal ridges indent the bones of my spine. Even the sky was angular. Then I saw that I was standing in the middle of a rectangle. Red paint had been daubed roughly onto the zinc, in the shape of posts and crossbar. They had brought me to a football pitch, to the goal-mouth. In the chabolas, we had played against just such a goal. At first, we had aimed at doorways, but this had incurred the wrath of coupling lovers who had been disturbed too often by the sudden entry from the alley of a flying, plastic bladder. So one day, someone had found a tin of red paint. Over the years, with millions of ball impacts, goalposts and crossbar had flaked and cracked and fallen to the ground. Yet they had never quite disappeared and were still there, a perfect geometric figure, when the bulldozers rolled in. Perhaps the soldiers too had battled against walls like these, yes, they were poor boys, I could see in the blacks of their eyes that certain fear which even after death never departs from the soul. Yet perhaps they had not been as skilled as I at the game and so while I, Acebo, had remained in the labyrinths of the chabolas and smashed my balls against the molten walls, they had put on uniforms and now fired a different kind of world.

One of the soldiers must have been an officer, because he produced a long-barrelled pistol from his hip. Undid the safety-catch. The sound of concrete on bone. Barked something at the other two, who promptly followed suit with their rifles. From somewhere, a cock crowed. The wall changed colour, from grey to red, and I knew that dawn had finally arrived. It filled my head with a buzzing sound. The three soldiers pointed their guns but they were no longer pointing at me. They were aiming for the goal-mouth. I could see that the left-hand one would miss completely. I wanted to tell him. After all, I was the better footballer. For years, I had swayed through the chabolas, looping spheres across the shifting roofs and shooting holy seed toward the sky. I raised my arms above my head. Between the bones, two birds danced an imperfect arc and then flew out of vision. I waited as the first streaks of red broke across the blue.

PYAR

Akbar Allegro had assumed the form of another word, of whose meaning I knew nothing. Even though my whole body was aching in some nightmare alchemy of lead, yet my diminutive pen slipped seamlessly across the paper and my right hand had warmed up. My left was still freezing, however, so I switched ends. You see, I am ambisextrous, I mean, ambidextrous and ambipedrous as well. I can hit with any of the four. Five, if you count my head.

But Old Akbar was off and running.

The centre circle of the pitch is our world; half-perfect, half-diabolic. The halfway line separates our consciousness from that of the other. The Game is about entering the internal (and external) world of another, and thereby beginning our journey towards our goal, towards illumination. Through physical love do we strive for spiritual, cosmic love. That's where Pyar comes in. Pyar is the Urdu word for romantic, human, physical love. It's an awkward word: PYAR. You have to get your tongue around it. To produce the correct sound you have to dribble the tip of your tongue over your hard palate at a certain frequency. You could never train a golem to say it. The love which may grow between human beings is always difficult; half-satanic, half-sublime; simultaneously selfish and selfless; it's a schizoid midfielder of a thing. It never knows whether to go for goal or to just be the backbone. It requires intelligence, adroitness, instinctive cunning. But it needs something more. Through the difficulty of the first phoneme, the field suddenly opens out at the end of the long, deformed aleph sound and we end on a note of satisfaction, satiety, post-orgasmic tranquillity. A long, rolling field 'rrr'. A classically Scottish 'rrr'. That's where most people stop, of course. A fag afterwards is their idea of spiritual enlightenment. The rising smoke, their deity. The ghosht of love, become music, is not the end; it is merely the means. The rhythm of the build-up suddenly falls apart; it just takes one pass to be less than perfect; and you're back in the void, chasing after comets in the darkness without border.

It is the hour of the witch, the moment of knowledge. By the trunk of the blackthorn tree, the Witch Queen holds between her teeth the balls of the kiss'd, blinded king of oak and she feels the life slip from his body and his shadow rushes to the rough ground beneath her feet. She lays him down on the fire, anoints herself with the salt of his skin, then leaps over the cauldron eightfold, once for each garter, and then in the green smoke of his flesh she begins to dance in a circle. She dances slowly at first like a molten stream, but with each deosil sweep of her white arm her feet move faster and faster until she is wheel-kicking over the arc of her skull and then in a moment of perfect circularity, the balls fly from the clamp of her jaw and whirl through the air, and land on her feet, each ball rolling on the tip of a big toe. And now, she, the balls and the wind swirl into a blur and occupy all points at once. It is total football.

Then she rises and flies as a wheel across the willow forest and the moors of red heather and the teeming city and she crosses the cold blue sea to the island of summer where words spiral in poetry up mountain-goat tracks. The octagonal House of Aradia welcomes her within its magic walls of cedar, sandalwood and juniper. Still cradling the balls of the King in the epidermal forest of her foot-skins, the witch eats the food of the dumb supper, she drinks from barrels of mead, she hears music which has no sound, no notes and she bathes in wine which evaporates slowly from her skin into the air. She is scourg'd by the tail'd cat and bleeds vines into the earth and as joyous fireflies pour down in light upon her, still she dances between the peaks of song.

At sunrise, she is whirling widdershins and her fingers have grown and lengthened and they pluck wrens from the boughs of ancient oak trees and the blood of the wrens feeds her belly which has bladder'd across the hog valley so that as her spine writhes in the dance, she lies down upon a blossom couch and from her raised, opened thighs, leap eleven wild women. And the women sing in a chorus-line:

Horse and hattock, horse and go!
Horse and pellatis, ho, ho, ho!

They sing this eleven times and their words raise a bone fire into the sky and the witch rocks on her rolling heels so that her feet become the long cone of a striker, head-to-boot, and the striker takes aim and shoots the balls of the King into the heart of the flames. The world stops. Breath ceases. The commentators in the pubs and prisons find themselves praying for the world. Then, from the heart of the fire, there leaps a giant, horn'd god. And the Witch Queen is unmoving as the beast lies down upon her and the two take up the chorea of electric blue moving stillness and their glowing transparency becomes a fiery line which cuts into the ground to form a spherical, glass altar. And through the glass, the Witch Queen sees the dark bone arch of the new moon, omphalos in the magenta sack of the sky. And in the black mirror of Idris, she calls and reads the scoreboards of all that has happened and everything that will come.

I checked myself to make certain that I had not sustained a long wet dream. Nope. All okay on that front.

Wow! Akbar-man, I said, somewhat breathlessly, Is that what you were thinking of when you scored the hat-trick against Strathclyde Police?

Listen, you idiot, it's about being possessed by a kind of a spirit, a duende, the Spanish might call it, or a succubus, if you like...

A succ... how d'you spell that?

But he was on a roll. He was dribbling and spinning and slipping between defenders. He was singing.

The anima which is inside every man and the animus within every woman.

I dig it, I really do.

I was somewhat lost. He was somewhere, far away and I wanted to be there.

Coming up through the tunnel, the hot concrete closes in on you and you feel as if you're going to suffocate and die there and never reach the pitch, let alone the trophy rank. It feels as though right at that moment the ball of the world is resting, on your shoulders. Your whole body trembles with fear or with something beyond fear.

Scottish Gas versus Parks and Maintenance? I ventured.

He shook his head.

It doesn't matter. The principle is the same. But once you have become filled with beauty there comes a certain white line which you must cross. If you baulk at this, you will remain a talented soccer player. The boundary between those who are merely talented and the truly great is indefinable. Tenuous. Yet they exist in different worlds, my friend. The second your studs hit turf, the moment you are out there, the blood pumps from the earth, up through the muscles of your legs, the quads, the hams, the buttocks, loins, right up through the fine coils of your brain, and you are out there, wheeling around the halfway circle and you are somewhere else. You're churning up the earth, digging deep, searching for the stream of gold.

But what about artificial turf?

My voice sounded hollow against the walls, as if nobody was there, in the cell.

Akbar impatiently waved away my question.

Beneath the turf is bedrock. That's all that counts.

His hand turned into a fist. For an insane moment, I thought he was about to punch me. Two symmetrical lines divided his forehead and the biceps and brachioradialis muscles of his right arm had swollen almost to bursting point. His eyes burned with such intensity, they were almost black. I could see then why this man had been the greatest player-manager the world had ever seen. How else could he have taken a team from a lonely Atlantean rock to the fire-

and-light belly of Cícero Pompeu de Toledo where with these same hands, he had held aloft the magic, golden cup.

Bedrock, I nodded.

He seemed to relax then. His features softened.

As a child, I had watched the old newsreel on TV. It had been my defining moment. I remembered that look on his face. The closed eyes, the expression of someone utterly, finally, at peace with himself and with the world. What I had seen through the glass of my television set, all those years back, was not the face of simple triumph. It was the visage of illumination. Now I knew why, in the lush valleys of the Gironde, Akbar had been known as 'Le Chansonnier', the songwriter, and from the swaying, blue littoral of the Maghreb, to the dust tracts of the Sahara, as 'El Said', the lord.

Yes. I said. I know.

But he just smiled dreamily and seemed to sink into a kind of torpor, so that he began to resemble one of those heavy-lidded, blue Hindu godlings which you see carved into the walls of temples and daubed across the frontages of multiplex cinemas. His form had become steadily less tangible as the night had worn on. But then, I hadn't actually stretched across the murk and touched his arm, so I couldn't really be sure.

He had other things on his mind and was keen to continue. I had run out of paper and so I began to write big on the walls.

If the passes work out, then the next obstacle is the semi-circle on the outside of the box. This is Aflatun's shadow world of ideal concepts. Only the sublime halves of our souls exist here. It mocks us from afar. Mocks our wars, our pestilences, our hopeless long-shots. And if we try short cuts, it penalises us mercilessly. That brings us to the ref and the goalie. Both are archangels. One dwelleth among us, sorting out our petty squabbles, dealing justice and injustice in equal measure (since how can we know justice unless we experience its opposite?), and sometimes, dealing death with a blood cipher. It must be a pretty depressing job. No wonder the Referee dresses in black. It takes a lot of pyar to get through this life, and not to despair of the garden. If you hog the ball, and not pass it on when you should, if you are driven by an excess of ego, then you will falter. You'll be shot on-target, a missed opportunity. A brilliant save! But for you, the glorious egotist, the flawed genius, there will be no salvation. That's where the goalie comes in. The penalty box is the goalie's stomping ground. It surrounds the original paradise which, in its turn, encircles heaven - the goal. Goalies are always different. Whichever archangel tossed us out of the beatific place now stands guard outside its walls. They have to be able to see, far and wide, to bounce and spring and slice and do everything in their power (which is almost, but not quite, total) to prevent us from sending that piece of ourselves, that devil's simulacrum of our world, that pig's bladder filled with holy breath, across the last boundary of this life.

OBITUARY NOTICE

ALLEGRO AKBAR.

Peacefully, after a long illness, at the Tree Tops Nursing Home, Maryhill, Glasgow. Beloved son of Madre Aradia and Padre Acebo, much loved bhai of Vittorio, dear father to Stanley, Manoel Francisco, Edson Arantes, Eusebio, Franz, Gerd, Bobby, Dennis, George, Alfredo, Diego, Ferenc, Michel, Zinedine, Johan, Lev and Sara. Funeral service, to which all friends and family are respectfully invited, at Cathcart Mosque, on Monday 21st June at 11am, thereafter to Hampden Park Stadium. No flowers please.

My pen had finally run out. I swore in eleven languages, I stamped and kicked with both feet simultaneously, managing, of course, not to fall over in the process, but nothing worked. Akbar Allegro was fading fast. With a wry expression on his face, he began to wave slowly at me and at what appeared to be an enormous crowd who en masse, were swaying their bodies back at him. Through the discordant roar of trumpet notes, he was mouthing words. Good job I could lip-read. One of the skills one learns, as a sports journo. Though usually, it would be multi-lingual expletives which one would be most expert at deciphering and those, you couldn't print.

Goodbye, adios, adieu, Khuda hafez, soraidh, auf wiedersehen, kalay shu, zai jian, arrivederla, gule gule...

I appealed to him:

Akbar, tell me, what would you have done in a tight situation like this? When you were right up against it, when you had to lead your team, Muckle Flugga United, against the serried ranks of Telecom Technik, the Kings of Faisalabad and the Lothian and Borders Water Company Limited or, once you had driven them like happy Carmelite Nuns, up the dank slope of League Double success, how had you arraigned the sloappie boays against the steeled Castilian might of Real Madrid?

But he just faded further into the rising dawn.

I was desperate. The Supers were wearing off. The crack was long fizzed out.

Akbar Allegro! Ni-o of the Red Chabolas! Witch Queen of the Northern Reaches! Pig's bladder concatenation of all our dead heroes and heroines! Help me score, just once before I die, help me be something better than myself! No flowers,

Pleeeeeeeezze!!!!!!

No reaction.

I felt my face pound with blood. I began to header my pen into the air in a frantic game of keepie-uppie. But it was hard, there, in the fading light with no black-cloaked referee and no car-coated stress-line manager about to crack down the middle with the incipient weight of a red-hot coronary. Have you ever tried it? Well, my advice would be: Don't. It was inevitable, in the same way that a penalty can be fated. You know what I mean. You can feel it coming, when you're really up against it, from somewhere in the marrow of your long-bones, you can just feel it coming.

Up
Up
Up
Up
Against
Against
Against the wall.

I fell to the floor, half-swooning, my scalp bleeding over my face like a stuck pig's bladder. I wasn't faking it, not here, not now, not in front of the Great Akbar Allegro's astral body. No sir, Ref., Man-in-Black. It was real. Real, real, real.

ISHQ

A brainwave. I would pen the final lines of Akbar Allegro on the prison wall in the Old Partick Police Station which like all the great games of this world, was no more. But more than that, I would quill the ultimate thought-forms of the world's number one crack shot in my own blood. A muscular arm helped me to my feet. I blinked, through the red waterfall, at the great man. He was making one last effort, one great sweep up front and he was doing it because up front is where miracles happen. Alchemy.

Ishq. The Arabic word for the highest, purest form of love. The love which can exist only between God and sentient being and which is transmuted, through breath, into immanence and transcendence, revelation and its opposite. The sound of the perfect shot. Ishq. The trajectory of the ball as it spins on its axis through the air, with the eyes of a million tripping lightly across its transfigured surface. With a football boot, with muscle, bone and breath, you can turn a sow's ear into a silk purse. A photon of love. The sound made by the 'i' is the intention, made real. The swing of the leg, the harmonic arc of the body, mirror the lines and curves of the field and the elegant, unseen fractals of the air. Aleph, undeformed. One. The long 'shhh' sweep of the ball through the sky. The last archangel knows that this time, you've managed to transfigure the kernel of yourself past the gates of the old, apple-green paradise and up, over the line of gnosis, into the vault of heaven's net. Qaaf. A fit way to end. Music from the deepest part of the vocal apparatus, from the throat's throat. And yet, that which is produced is not guttural, but sibilant almost like the pure note which lies somewhere within Middle C. The sound of the ball as it strikes the net. Zidane. Hampden. 15th May 2002. 45th minute. A sound which, amidst the alleluia epiphany of the oceanic roar, is never heard, except by those who know. Huu.

So singing, Akbar Allegro, Master of the Midfield Dribble, Shah-en-Shah of the scimitar strike, Royal Duke of Angular Delusional Defence techniques, singer-songwriter, Barón of the Chabolas, invisible dance-partner of all the aspiring, perspiring greats, magian of the winger's impossibly long sweep and Queen Witch of himself, vanished into thin air.

A rattling of keys at the door.

The moon, the cell window, the cell itself, all had disappeared. This place no longer existed and so whoever was at the door was not a good old, dear blue police constable, but something else altogether. Perhaps it was the Soccer Satan, the relegated angel, but then that would mean that I was in the Ninth Division of Hell. I closed my eyes, took a single, circular, deep breath and then held it taut, within me. I held the air inside my chest for as long as I possibly could, longer than I had ever before managed. I held it in for so long that flecks of light began to dance between the dark, inner skin of my lids and the moist globules that were my eyes. I held the ball of breath in my lungs for so long that they began to swell and my chest, to expand. I grew bigger and bigger until I came to fill the darkness of the Old Partick Police Station, of the Dear Green Place, of the cold, white land, of the geo-harmonic entity known as Eurasia and finally of the great big, soft leather ball of the world.

Then I let out my breath. Opened my eyes.

The sky is a huge blue oval. Below the sky, people. Lots of them. Thousands, maybe millions. Tiny faces, of all colours, and each one is yelling, singing, burping, blowing on a tin bugle or just dreaming. Only in the Elite Presidential Box, are the voices silent, the faces, empty.

The stadium is like a funnel, siphoning the crowd into a hum around my head, a single note which becomes the pulse of blood through my brain. My body arcs across the centre spot. In the far distance, the tiny rectangle of the goal. Now it is all so clear. No wood. Twenty-one other players on the field; two and one is three. The ball, the goal and me. Ghosht, pyar, ishq. I have relinquished the role of voyeur; I have stretched beyond myself. The fractal of the pitch pullulates in my brain in a rhythm which like all rhythms, is beyond words.

I draw the studs of my heel backward in a slow arc across the bright green astroturf and then tap, hard, once, twice, thrice. My ritual. To measure out the space, to fire my own personal sonar down towards bedrock. On my right arm is wound the Captain's band. In my eyes, burn the madness of the black fire. And over to my left, a solemn man in a black cloak. He raises his hand to his face. Om. Tattva. Baraka.

The whistle blows. The air smells good today.

In loving memory of Sameena Jamil, aka 'Queen Jamila' (1982–2001)

The Tomintoul Deliverance

Brian Hennigan

The game of life
has no goalposts,
much less a
half-time whistle.

The game of life has no goalposts, much less a half-time whistle. And while there are those who sneak the odd ten yards here and there, for most of us it is a case of being caught offside with each and every apparently salvatory through ball. It is a common jest that when it comes to ill-gotten gain, God has no Russian linesmen. So that when – as the last days of life start to appear – and we recognise that that was very much that, few of us can recall with any truth the glory of a truly miraculous day. But I can.

Those shiny months of long ago seemed at the time no different from any other. Their names were the same then as they are now; June, July, August. Or the Months of Leather, as we called them in the village of Loch Muick. For the joy of football brings much respite to the long days of Highland summer. No sooner has the last stone of winter been curled than the men of the village assume fixed positions in the pub, there to talk up the omens of the coming season. And when that particular season arrived, it brought a message of severe concern.

While for most football was first and foremost a diversion, a game, a distracting act of physical fancy, there could be no doubt that an element of serious-mindedness had snuck onto the field of late. While previously the aim had been purely to recapture that sense of innocent fun known only to the young and certain train drivers, there was now little doubt that the point of each match was to win and to win at all costs. In no situation was this more apparent than in the yearly contest for inter-glen supremacy played out by rival teams of crofters; the so-called Tenant's Cup.

While affecting our usual nonchalance for the occasion, there could be no doubting the sense of trepidation that affected our movement like a soggy sweater as we waited news of that year's draw. Sitting at the foot of the valley, we watched as hilltop after hilltop carried fiery news of the teams being drawn. No sooner had our own wooden pyre been set ablaze than down the slope rushed Fast Jacob, the local conveyer of bad news. In his hand was a mildly scorched envelope, which – as custom dictated – he threw to the ground in front of me, honorary captain for the season. As custom dictated I picked up the envelope, opened it, and read aloud the words

'Loch Muick will play...'

Immediately Fast Jacob raced back up the hill, returning with another mildly scorched envelope.

'Athletico Tomintoul.'

Ah, the ancient enemy.

The rivalry between the Loch Muick and Tomintoul stretches to the very suburbs of time. Yet only once in living memory had the two teams been drawn against each other, and the land still shook with fizzy torpor in recollection of that malevolent encounter. We had won that day, but that was long ago. In those distant days we had been masters of the flighted ball in the air, followed by a ten man charge into the penalty area. None could resist the Loch Muick Scramble.

In those days the boys of Tomintoul had proven easy baps for the men of our town. Yet over the years there had been a gradual erosion of our footballing power. First the rules were enforced, nullifying our assault-based strategy. Then, the game itself had changed, as man after man fell to the notion of passing the ball between them, each ground-based stroke bringing calamity to our air-based stratagem.

As the night air began to cling to our limbs like a damp towel of doom, so our hearts felt heavy at the prospect of the inevitable capitulation to Athletico Tomintoul. Gathering at the feet of the Bob 'the Goat' McPherson, architect of that long ago victory, we reconciled ourselves to do our best while expecting the worst.

That night as I lay under the duvet, I was unable to sleep. My wife suggested turning off the television, but even then my mind seemed ill at ease. Rising in the early hours I was drawn to the front window, from where I was able to look down on Bob's statue, outlined in the brittle mist of the morning. Considering his impassioned grimace, I knew there and then that we could not, must not lose the coming match. At the same time, how would we win?

I was on my way back from borrowing that morning's paper when there was a chill, alien wind on the street, followed by a silence of unusual portent. Turning, I saw that the bus had arrived. As it drew away, pursued by the usual crowd of asylum seeking housewives, I

p48
The figure pirouettes to catch t

bounce against his lower back.

noticed a figure standing on the pavement, bathed in a tracksuit of unusual hue.

As I saw him, he saw me. With a jaunty step he strode over and held out his hand,

'Hello, I understand there is a football match to prepare for.'

'Yes there is,' I replied, shaking his non-clipboard holding hand. 'But first I've got to get the milk and bread.'

So it was that a figure to this day known only as The Manager arrived in Loch Muick. You can see his bronze bust next to the nine items or less queue. Yet that morning I had time for only two items and once they had been safely delivered The Manager was on to me again, and a squad meeting was arranged for that evening.

As the team sat round him on the pitch, impervious to the heavy rain and the ladies hockey match raging all around, we listened as he explained how we were going to win the match against Athletico Tomintoul.

What followed over those short few weeks – reduced to six days in order to maximise the amount of training – was little less than a revelation. Never had one man placed so much emphasis on the team, the team, the team. Soon we had ceased to think as individuals and become an unstoppable footballing zombie army. This resulted in many of the schools being shut and a special service being said, while The Manager went over again what he had meant by thinking and acting in unison.

More important still were the minor changes he effected. No longer was drinking on the pitch permitted, even at throw-ins. And while few quibbled with most of these alterations, some proved problematic. The introduction of the so-called Continental System was too much for many. Unable to get baguettes for breakfast, they were forced to tie three rolls together, one of which always fell off into the porridge.

As the first game of the new era approached, our confidence was at an all time high. Which was strange as we were thrashed 9–0 by Dynamo Fochabers. Indeed, as the season wore on, the positive outcome of our training seemed difficult to discern when it came to match day. And while the defeat to Sporting Kilwhinnie was a disappointment, it was as nothing to the shaming by Unsporting Kilwhinnie, who not only scored five times but also hid our boots and called us names.

Yet throughout this all we stood by The Manager, because we knew deep down that the results on the field were up to us. Which was when The Manager decided to change what 'us' meant?

It is important, he explained, that we use the best people we have, regardless of background. As an example, he arrived one day at training with the fishmonger, Patrick, and his brothers Seamus and Michael.

'Now then, do you know what's different about these three?' The Manager asked. Silent, we waited for explanation

'They kick,' he informed us, tapping his nose. 'With the left foot'.

As one we gasped aloud. It was obvious what that meant. They would all be uniquely adept at passing or crossing the ball from the left side. Given this skill, we felt it best that Patrick, Seamus and Michael be given a bit of extra space in the dressing room. Indeed, we went so far as to offer them their own.

Yet although the addition of new squad members improved our options and helped boost morale further, there was little improvement in results. As the big day against Athletico Tomintoul dawned, few of us woke with any form of optimism. Some didn't even have a pillow.

Despite our run of form, there was still a huge turn-out for the game. A festive atmosphere had seized the village, and it was almost impossible to move for Christmas trees. A more sombre note was provided by the death from premature excitement of the team sponsor, Aly MacFadden, owner of MacFadden's Ice Creams. As a mark of respect the squad drove up and down the touchline prior to kick-off balanced in pyramid formation atop an ice-cream van while the local girl guides played By The Rivers of Babylon on xylophones. From the Chairman's Box, Mrs MacFadden waved us on, a tear in her eye, a cone in her hand. The whistle for kick-off heralded not so much a beginning as an end; our end it seemed. From the off we were subjected to wave after wave of pummeling football that threatened to have us going into the interval with double figures against us. It was only the adoption of our 9–0–1 formation that prevented such a tragedy. I was playing upfront, supported by a virtual midfield, with the massed defence tossing such long bangers up to me as they could. As it was, we were lucky to reach the 45 minute mark without a goal being scored.

Yet on the long walk to the dressing room the words DEFEAT HUMILIATION DISHONOUR hung over us like a sign from the almighty, although it turned out to be a plane trailing a banner paid for by a Tomintoul supporter.

'You're not going to win by not playing football,' The Manager implored us. None of us could deny that, although several tried and soon discovered the perils of the double-negative. And then we were back out on the pitch. It happened so quickly that many of us still had our half-time oranges. One or two hadn't even finished their half-time kebabs.

Thus the siege continued. Football is a game of two halves. Or one, as we used to say, one.

And there was a clear unity between the first half and the second half as our opponents set about us with malevolent glee. On and on they came and each time they were repelled. It was at times reminiscent of the film Zulu, particularly when the Tomintoul attack set fire to the thatched roof of our goal.

In some respects we thought that the game might never end, that this was to be our own personal limbo, with our footballing souls left to play out eternity against the devils from beyond the next Glen. As the forty-fourth minute approached, it became clear that this sense of angst had spread to the stands. The full-time pitch invasion was about to start and not everyone was in the mood for extra-time. Many were on their knees in prayer and emergency pies were being handed out.

Then, in the next to last gasp of the game, something happened. The Tomintoul midfield had once more been handed possession on our 18 yard line, when a call from our Manager, broke through the tumult.

'Keep at it lads. It isn't over until the fat lady sings!'

This revelation – familiar to all of us who had participated in The

Manager's training sessions – stunned the players and fans of Athletico Tomintoul to a man. They had until that point been waiting for a whistle to end the contest. As their eyes turned to Mrs MacFadden – whose ice-cream-based figure seemed to be the fattest on show – I raced back and took the ball off the toes of their centre-half. Spurting forward, there was no holding my feet as I danced towards their goal. Waiting for the goalkeeper to commit himself I then launched a mighty drive past his flailing figure. The ground erupted and I remember no more.

Too often a wander down memory lane turns into a forced march down Nightmare Avenue. I am grateful to have one particular day that is etched in gold in many minds, and in ballpoint on many desks. It was one of those days that seemed it would last forever. So that at the stroke of midnight there was a profound sense of shock and disbelief. None more so than among the followers and team of Athletico Tomintoul, who retreated to their buses and sang no more, a point we felt compelled to remind them of until their drive home began.

And at the end – long after our own supporters had gathered their and others belongings and headed home, only we remained by the statue of Bob 'the Goat' McPherson. A team of footballers, lead by a man for whom victory was a seven letter word.

Of that man there was nothing to be seen. Some speculated that he had been kidnapped, others that they saw his puce form ambling out of town some moments after the match concluded. For me, I know he is out there somewhere, bringing tactics to the tactless and know-how to the know-howless. And every now and then – when I hear the sound of one hand clapping – I know it is him.

The Last Man in Scotland Who Doesn't Like Football

Colin Clark

You'd think it was some sort of crime no to like football in this fuckin country.

'It was the final straw, Your Honour. The final fuckin straw,' he says, face hangin like a wet towel. I thought he was goin to start to greet.

'Yes, it was a terrible thing, Your Honour. No, Your Honour, I'm no shirkin my responsibility. I don't think I'm a menace to society,' he says, 'though others have tried to drag my name through the mud. I'm fully aware of the seriousness of my actions but I want to plead mitigatin circumstances.'

Mitigatin circumstances! What mitigatin circumstances? No likin football? Poor bastard.

Aye, I was at the sports centre, saw the whole thing. A bad business. Like he said, the final fuckin straw. One last ignominy. Blootered by a wet bladder, right on the coupon. No that he seen it comin, right enough. No that he could've done nothin about it if he had. You can just picture him, first catchin it in the corner of his eye goin, 'oh fuck!', seein this great muddy orb, floatin in the sky like a Dundee sunset, then actually catchin it smack right in the eye.

Must have been sore right enough. You can just see him, eh. No feelin it connect, but feelin the sting of it after. Clothes all muddy, face all sore, and him that pissed off with it all. Every bastard laughin.

Alan Hastie. That's right. I knew him from primary. He'd never been one for the football. He just wasny built for it. He was a snivelly wee bastard. A right wee runt. *Pasty Hastie* we called him. I mind him playin it at school. He was always shite, but. His dad – no his real dad, by the way (there were doubts about his parentage), I think it was his stepdad or something – well, he bought him one of they orange Mitres for his birthday one year, though fuck knows why. He came in all proud with it under his arm, still shiny, no been touched. The Mitre was a cool ball in they days, no many folk had one. I think he wanted one so's he could be one of the boys.

No, no. Don't get me wrong, Hastie was a hell of a nice guy, a wee bit quiet. He just didny have any pals. Anyway, the day Alan brought his Mitre into school it stayed in his possession till about lunchtime when it got requisitioned into service in the primary fours versus the primary fives. Hastie got a game cos it was his ball, but we put him in goal cos he was fuck all use anywhere else. At some point one of the primary fives had a clear shot at Hastie's goal and belted it. You should have seen his face. We're all shouting, 'come out and meet him, watch your angles!'

But he just stood there rooted to the spot, shitin himself, and this big bastard, Mackay I think his name was, toes it right at him. Maybe if he'd put his hands up or ran out to him it wouldny have been so bad. But as it was, wee Hastie got the full impact right smack on the nose. The ball bounced back and one of the other primary fives took a shot but he skied it and it ended up on the school roof just as the bell went.

We all trooped in and just left it up there. We sat in Mr McCafferty's room pishin ourselves watchin wee Hastie tryin to shin up the drainpipe. Ended up in front of the Head.

The ball? Oh aye, eh, I think one of the primary sevens went up after school and claimed it. I don't remember. Shame, but with that business down the sports centre I think that moment kind of set the course for the rest of his life.

I don't know, maybe it was the concussion, maybe it was the humiliation. Maybe it was a combination of things. But from then on wee Hastie just wasny into football any more. Funny enough, that game was probably the one time Hastie actually saved a goal in his puff.

Secondary school, aye. I had him in my English class for a couple of years. We had this sarcastic bastard for a teacher. His patter was quite funny but he could be right nasty. Wee Hastie got it every fuckin week.

Well, he started playin clarinet when he got into first year, you see. Totally askin for trouble: no being into football *and* playin an instrument. Got some pelters for it. It's a sin for him when you look back but school was like that. The law of the jungle.

Matters werny helped by this sarky English teacher who took the total pish out of him for goin to music lessons.

'Are you goin to blow your horn, Alan. How do you manage?' he'd say. And stuff like, 'Is that you away to fiddle with your instrument again? You'll go blind.' With this totally camp voice. His other one was, 'Alan's away to tweak the licorice stick watch it doesny drip all over you, now.'

I'd be sniggerin away with the rest of them watchin the poor guy try to squeeze his way through rows of desks. I don't think his musical career lasted much beyond third year. He ended up with the same bastard teacher again who called him *The Licorice Licker* the whole year.

Aye, PE was worse, obviously.

No, the PE teacher was alright, there wereny any vicious bastards in PE, I don't think. They were usually all up in Maths and Geography. And English, obviously. The trouble with PE was it was always football for the boys, netball for the girls, so you were fucked if you were rubbish at it.

The trouble, though, with this teacher was he was just really unobservant. You see, Wee Alan was never given the relative saftey of goal in PE, he was always out with the bears getting hacked to fuck every time the teacher's back was turned. I suppose the teacher was only doin his best, tryin to develop our skills in different positions instead of havin the usual cunts always defendin and the showoffs always up front. Alan's mistake was no bein into it. He didny even watch the game on the telly. Maybe if he'd just pretended or somethin.

Well, the perverse logic of PE teachers made it Alan was always on the pitch. I think the teacher thought wee Hastie'd develop a likin for the game if he just played it more often. All that happened of course was that every time the ball came near him Alan would either duck or run the opposite way which meant he always got blamed for any goals that were lost. Which is fair enough, cos he *was* shite.

I know, I know. But I'll tell you this, see people that don't like football. I just don't get it. Do you? I mean, it's just – well, it's no natural. Know what I'm sayin. You just have to walk through town on a Saturday when the Old Firm's playin: nobody for miles. Anybody who says he doesny like football's a lying bastard. Though now I think about it, there's wee Hastie. I suppose you can understand to an extent, but you see the mess he's got himself into now. You think he'd have realised.

No, he never learned. Wait till you hear this. One of the guys I play fives with's got a boy up at the secondary. Apparently Hastie's teachin up there now.

Aye, straight up. And guess what he's teachin...

Naw, no PE. But close on the masochistic stakes.

Aye, English.

Fucked up intit! You'd think he'd want to give schools a bodyswerve. I don't think there's a man born who had a more miserable time when he was at school. And they say they're the happiest days of your life. Maybe he's after a second go.

Well, the reason we found out is this pal of mine's wasny happy about who was teachin his boy.

There were, eh – rumours.

It all started when a punishment exercise went home. His boy had called this new teacher *Bawheid* to his face. Weans'll find names for anybody. Everyone agreed it was the teacher's fault for no bein able to control his class so it was all forgotten for a bit. Then they started sayin the guy was a poof. Nothin wrong with that, some of my best friends are poofs. But stories started to come out that, like, this guy wasny just a poof, but a poof that liked wee boys. As you can imagine, my pal was more than a wee bit concerned so he went up to talk to the guidance teacher and it turns out this pervert was Hastie.

Ach, you know what weans are like. Apparently the class asked him what team he supported and he told them he didny like football. Stands to reason: doesny like football, *must* be a poof.

That's what I thought. But then that got exaggerated and he starts bein called a child molester and, what with the papers full of stories about paedophiles, that just gave them another name they could call him.

I remember that. You journalists, you've a fuck of a lot to answer for.

Anyway, it turns out about a few weeks before the business at the sports centre he'd got a call from the Head. He'd kept hearin these stories about Hastie fiddlin with boys in his cupboard, droppin his trousers in the underpass at primary kids, askin first years to let him feel their arses in return for good marks. A load of pish. Just weans havin a laugh, spreadin malicious rumours and that. Hastie goes up to the Head's office and the cops are there to arrest him on suspicion of indecent exposure. At the end of the day, though, they canny pin fuck all on him; he denies it, the weans willny testify cos the bastards made it up, and nothin can be proven either way. So they suspend him on full pay until the shite settles.

Of course the shite doesny settle. With all the hype about paedophiles he has vigilantes outside his door smearing shite on his windows and all the middle class parents askin the council to put him on the transfer list. It was just after that there was the carry on down the sports centre.

Aye, I saw the whole thing. I was watchin the junior quarter-final. My wee nephew's one of the star players.

What happened? Well, it was all a bit sudden. One of the defenders from the other team belts a penalty right over the bar and out the park and it lamps this poor bastard who's walkin past the pitch.

I don't know, maybe he was comin back from the country park. There's a nature walk down there. Anyway, the ball lands right on top of this guy and knocks him into the mud, glasses flyin in two different directions. He's no very happy about it and starts paintin the air blue with insults. I don't know if he could see that he was swearin at wee laddies, but some of the parents and myself included werny that chuffed at the language he was usin. Before we could go down and sort him out one of the boys had went over to ask for the ball back and this sets him off.

What? Aye, that's right!

He starts shoutin, 'You want your fuckin ball back? You want your fuckin ball back? Here's your fuckin ball!'

And he chucks it into the air like he's goin to sky it for miles. Unfortunately, the daft cunt, it bounces off his shin and lands a few feet away. That's when we recognise him. The guy who's in my five a side team spots him first. Word goes around and the mood gets ugly. Folk seemed to have forgotten he was cleared of they paedophile allegations.

'Ya shower a fuckin bastards!' he shouts back.

Then he takes a run at the ball and swipes at it with his foot. This time his foot connects with the ball and sails it spectacularly out the sports ground over the hedge by the main road. Best shot I've ever seen him take.

'There's your fuckin ball!' he shouts and gives us the vicky and makes off sharpish. He doesny get more than a couple of yards though cos that's when the double decker ploughs through the hedge into the sports ground, a muddy splat decoratin the driver's side of the windscreen where the ball's hit it, and the Nissan Micra danglin off the front bumper.

No, nobody seriously hurt, but aye, that's right, 5 years custodial sentence. Reckless endangerment or somethin.

Last thing I heard him say before he went down was, 'You'd think it was some sort of crime no to like football in this fuckin country.'

Well, aye, nice talkin to you too. You spelt my name right, by the way?

Author Biographies

Alan Spence is an award-winning poet and playwright, novelist and short story writer. Books include *The Magic Flute, Stone Garden, Way to Go* and *Glasgow Zen*. He is currently Professor in Creative Writing at the University of Aberdeen.

Bernard MacLaverty was born in Belfast but in the 70 ' s moved to Scotland to teach. After living in Edinburgh and Islay, he now lives in Glasgow. He has published four collections of short stories and four novels.

Linda Cracknell won the Macallan/Scotland on Sunday short story competition in 1998. Since then she has published a short story collection, *Life Drawing*. She is now working on a novel and writing radio drama.

Laura Hird was born and lives in Edinburgh. Her novel, *Born Free*, short story collection, *Nail and Other Stories* and two novellas were published by Canongate Books. Further publications are in the pipeline.

Iain Maloney hails from Aberdeen and is a recent graduate in English from the University of Aberdeen where he has been heavily involved in creative writing and amateur dramatics. His first collection of poetry, *Fences We Build*, was published in 1999.

Gordon Legge was born in Falkirk and brought up in Grangemouth. He has published four books, the most recent being *Near Neighbours* published by Vintage. He is presently working on a novel.

Jim Carruthers was born in Dumfriesshire in 1954. With his wife and three children, Jim now lives near Perth where he gardens professionally. *The Cherrypicker* was written in a snowbound tractorshed. Jim's interests include Dundee United.

Andrew C Ferguson is 39, married with one daughter, and lives in Glenrothes. A co-written non-fiction book, *Legacy of the Sacred Chalice*, was published earlier this year. His poetry and short fiction has been published in various mainstream and genre magazines.

Billy Cornwall was born Leith 1958, a Hibby godloveus. He has been a labourer, a tutor, and editor/dogsbody with various publications. Previous work published in: Rebel Inc., West Coast and various others.

Des Dillon was born 1960 and brought up in Coatbridge, Lanarkshire. He studied English at Strathclyde University, taught English and was the Writer in Residence in Castlemilk 1998-2000. He lives in Galloway.

Alan Bissett was born in Falkirk in 1975. He lives in Leeds. His first novel *boyracers* was published last year by Polygon.

Denise Mina went to Glasgow University to study law, having previously completed a series of McJobs. In a shoddy misuse of her PhD grant, she wrote her first novel *Garnethill* while dodging other responsibilities. *Garnethill* won the CWA Gold Dagger for the best first novel. *Exile* and *Resolution* completed the trilogy and her first stand-alone novel *Sanctum* was published in November 2002.

Suhayl Saadi is an award-winning writer whose book, *The Burning Mirror* was short-listed for the Saltire First Book Prize. His novel, *Kings of the Dark House*, is due out in 2002. More information from www.suhaylsaadi.com.

Brian Hennigan is author of *Patrick Robertson: A Tale of Adventure* published by Jonathan Cape. He has twice been short-listed for the Macallan Short Story Prize and his fiction has been widely published or broadcast.

Colin Clark is a writer and teacher. He lives in Glasgow and is a student on the Creative Writing MPhil at Glasgow University.

Freight Design is a Glasgow-based design consultancy with a passion for football, literature and doing our own thing. *The Hope That Kills Us* is the bastard spawn of Freight's founding directors, Adrian Searle and Davinder Samrai.

Permissions

The Thing About Brazil © Alan Spence 2002

A Belfast Memory © Bernard MacLaverty 2002

The Match © Linda Cracknell 2002

This Is My Story, This Is My Life © Laura Hird 2002

Football Scarves and Richard Kimble © Iain Maloney 2002

The Hand of God Squad © Gordon Legge 2002

The Cherrypicker © Jim Carruthers 2002

Nae Cunt Said Anyhin © Andrew C Ferguson 2002

Jesus Saves © Billy Cornwall 2002

Heatherstone's Question © Des Dillon 2002

A Minute's Silence © Alan Bissett 2002

The Bigot © Denise Mina 2002

Sufisticated Football © Suhayl Saadi 2002

The Tomintoul Deliverance © Brian Hennigan 2003

The Last Man Left In Scotland Who Doesn't Like Football © Colin Clark 2002

DESIGN © **FREIGHT**